CHAPTER 1 3

CHAPTER 2 7

CHAPTER 3 12

CHAPTER 4 17

CHAPTER 5 22

CHAPTER 6 28

CHAPTER 7 35

CHAPTER 8 40

CHAPTER 9 45

CHAPTER 10 52

CHAPTER 11 58

CHAPTER 12 64

CHAPTER 13 70

CHAPTER 14 76

CHAPTER 15 79

CHAPTER 16 86

CHAPTER 17 91

CHAPTER 18 96

CHAPTER 19 101

CHAPTER 20 105

CHAPTER 21 109

CHAPTER 22 114

CHAPTER 23 120

CHAPTER 24 124

Chapter 1

It was the 22nd of July and Thea was led on her bed, staring at the ceiling. Well, she was led on just her mattress, as her bed frame had already been dismantled and packed, ready for the move. Her gaze went from the ceiling, to the bare walls, to the bin bags of clothes piled high in the corner of the room. She sat up, sighed heavily, looking at the rest of her belongings that should really be in boxes already. She slumped off the mattress and wandered over to her mirror, stood on her tiptoes and began to glance at herself.

Thea was a great deal shorter than all the other fourteen year olds in her school. A petite girl with long black glossy hair and soft pastel skin. She was nice to look at, but did not often dress like all the other girls her age. Thea was quite content wearing oversized jumpers, baggy jeans and mostly liked to stick her hair up into a messy loose bun.

Although staring at herself, hoping she would grow a few inches within the next ten minutes, was fascinating, she knew her worldly goods would not box themselves. Her mum had shown her how to place things properly within the boxes, making items fit nicely together like a well played game of tetris, but Thea had quickly given up on the art of packing and continued to throw things in the boxes, hoping her mum would not check.

She had just about finished flinging her possessions into boxes, when she received a text message from her best friend, Sarah. Thea was going to miss Sarah more than anyone else she knew in London. Sarah had been her closest friend for the last 6 years, and Thea was still finding it difficult to comprehend a new life without her. Her mum tried to comfort her, explaining that Sarah would only be a five hour drive away, but Thea was used to having Sarah living only two roads away.

Thea didn't read the text from Sarah straight away. Instead she sat staring at her phone, already trying to hold back tears, knowing the message would just set her off again.

She looked around her bedroom again. The only bedroom she had ever known. The new house was not a strange house, in fact it was basically her second home, but she never imagined it would be her only home. Thea's Grandpa had passed away just over a year ago, and her Grandma was not coping too well living on her own, although she never liked to show it. The family all knew Grandma Maisy would never leave her home, especially to come and live in London, so the only option was to all bundle in with her. Thea had always wanted a little brother or sister in the past, but was quite relieved now, as she would have had to share a room with them in Grandma Maisy's house.

She saw her phone was still flashing. She took a deep breath and read the message from Sarah.

Stay strong, Batty.

Thea smiled to herself. Sarah had not called her Batty in quite some time. A nickname that was created by Sarah, due to Thea's dark hair, pale skin and ability to stay up all night, usually painting or reading. Sarah had thought Batty sounded cuter than just calling her best friend an outright Vampire. Thea's dad had caught on to the nickname for a while, often calling her 'Tatty Batty', when he saw her dressed in her paint covered clothes with her hair in the messy bun, most of it sticking out all over the place.

Thea started to tape up the last boxes when her mum appeared at her bedroom door.

"How are we getting on?" her mum asked, in quite an excited manor. Her mum had tried her best to make the move sound as exhilarating as possible for weeks.

"Fine mum." Thea replied. "I am just taping up the last of the boxes."

"Ok well you best get to bed soon. We are leaving bang on 7am tomorrow."

Thea continued to tape up the boxes, knowing full well she would not be getting much sleep that night.

"Have you heard from Sarah today?" her mum asked, speaking in a much softer tone this time.

Thea stopped, glared at her mum and felt her eyes starting to water. She shrugged her shoulders and immediately looked back down at the boxes.

"Right, well then," her mum continued, "I shall leave you to it. Goodnight Tee."

"Night mum."

Thea's mum left the room. Thea sauntered over to her window and gazed at the beautiful night time scenery London had on offer. She would miss this view. A lot of her paintings were inspired by the city skylines. Soon all she would have to paint was trees, grass and cows. She always enjoyed visiting Grandma Maisy, mainly because she missed her Grandma a lot, but she was never thrilled about the long family hikes and eating lunch, sitting on the dirty ground in the woods.

The worst thing about this move was her parents' impeccable timing. The summer holidays had only just started, meaning Thea's chance of finding friends anytime soon was slim to none. She wasn't too bothered about having to start a new school, she found making friends quite easy, but she already knew she would not find another Sarah.

She grabbed her phone and sat back on her mattress. She stared at the message from Sarah, trying to think of a reply that did not sound too gushy. In all honesty, she wanted to tell Sarah she would miss her more than anything, and that they should pack their bags and get a train to anywhere, and start a new life on their own. Thea giggled to herself thinking about it. Thea and Sarah had once set off the smoke alarm at school with their awful cooking skills, so they had always joked about how they would have to live off sandwiches and chocolate bars if they ever lived together when they were older.

She put her phone down on the floor, without replying. She got into her pyjamas, the only belonging of hers not hidden away in a box, turned out the light and slumped down under the duvet. She still couldn't quite believe this would be her last night in this house forever. She had seen the new buyer a couple of weeks ago. A single mum with three very noisy young boys. Thea hoped the lady would not change the house too much. The house was a Victorian building and her parents had kept as many original features as they could. Each room, including her bedroom, had beautiful original fireplaces. Her mum had kept the original wallpaper in the study downstairs. A delicate fleur de lis pattern in gold, with a duck egg surround. Thea couldn't bear the thought of the wallpaper ever being torn down, or the fireplaces being ripped out. She started to cry again. She felt so selfish, feeling like this, when she knew her Grandma needed her family, and that it was only a house, but it was her home. She carried on crying until she must have finally fallen asleep. Her alarm went off at 6am, startling her slightly. Thea laid on her back, closed her eyes and whispered to herself.

"*Moving day*".

Chapter 2

"Tee!" her mum shouted from the bottom of the stairs. "Tee! Are you up?"

"Yes mum!" she replied, a lot less enthusiastically. Thea sat up and grabbed her rucksack and pulled out her toothbrush, toothpaste and deodorant. The only things she had managed to salvage before her mum rampaged the bathroom. She had also remembered to leave herself a pair of clean knickers. She dressed herself in the same clothes from the day before and packed her pyjamas into her rucksack.

"Tee, come down and get something to eat, Dad has got all of us bacon rolls from the cafe." Thea was still not looking forward to any part of this day, but even she could not say no to a bacon roll. She looked around her room one last time, focusing on the little marks on the walls from the tape that once held up her posters and the stain on the carpet from where Sarah had once made her laugh so much, cola had shot out of her nose. She sighed deeply, took a deep breath and left her room, closing the door behind her.

She did not realise how hungry she was until she saw that bacon roll. Within only a few minutes it was gone.

"Blimey, did you even taste any of that?" Thea's mum muttered.

"Oh let her enjoy it, Sue!" her dad replied.

Thea's dad was smiling at her. A very sympathetic smile, but warming.

"The movers will go up and get our mattresses and the rest of our boxes when we have left." her mum explained, looking a little anxious.

"Don't worry Sue, we have hired professionals. We have all the breakables in our car anyway." her dad assured.

"Yes, yes I know. Tee, have you got everything you need for the journey?"

"Why? What do I need?" she replied, looking confused.

"Well I thought you might like to bring your sketchbook. Five hours is a long time to be in the car."

"It is quite hard to draw something when you shoot past it at eighty miles per hour, Mum."

Her dad sniggered from behind his paper.

"Do not encourage her stroppiness, Kevin! Today will be stressful enough without you two ganging up on me."

She watched her mum fetch bottles of water from the fridge and put them in a cool bag for the trip, along with some apples and cereal bars.

"Dad, will we stop somewhere and get a proper lunch?" she whispered.

"Yes, don't worry. You know your mother never leaves the house without snacks, whether the drive is 5 hours or 5 minutes."

"Right!" her mum cried out, startling both Thea and her dad, "Let's get a move on! Thea, your jacket is on the stairs."

Thea put on her jacket and grabbed her rucksack.

"Goodbye kitchen, goodbye lounge, goodbye bathroom, bedrooms and stairs! Goodbye London!" her dad bellowed.

Suddenly Thea felt very sick, and the after taste of the greasy bacon in her mouth was not helping. This move was actually happening and it was happening now.

Thea stood and looked up at the house from the front garden. "Goodbye house." she whispered, and reluctantly got into the car.

"Are we all strapped in?" her mum asked from the driver's seat.

"Yes, mum." replied both Thea and her dad. Her mum glared at them both.

"Right then, off we go on our new adventure!"

Thea watched as her beloved home grew further and further away, until she could no longer see it at all. A tear rolled down her cheek.

"So, Tee" her mum began "your birthday is only a few weeks away. Any ideas on what you would like yet?"

Thea was surprised at her mum's choice of topic. She had literally just been taken away from her home and her friends, and her mum really thought she wanted to think about her birthday? A birthday without Sarah.

"I really don't know mum. Maybe some new paints? I am running low on quite a few colours actually."

"Oh wouldn't you prefer some nice new clothes, a dress maybe? Or some makeup? Something a bit more girly."

Thea rolled her eyes.

"I saw that in the mirror, Tee!" her mum cried.

"Sue, if you think Tee needs a dress and some makeup to be a girl, you are stuck further in the past than your mother."

Thea's mum rolled her eyes.

"I saw *that* in the mirror, mum."

Thea's dad tried not to smile, but he was not doing a very good job of hiding it. Her mum turned up the radio, which was an obvious sign the conversation was over.

"I think I am going to try and get some sleep, I still feel very tired." Thea yawned.

"I did bring some small pillows for the trip." her dad said, handing Thea a pillow for herself.

Thea tucked the pillow under her head and drifted off a lot easier than expected.

She was awoken a little while later by her dad shaking her leg.

"Wake up Tee, let's get some food."

She slowly opened her eyes and saw they had made a pit stop at a petrol station. She looked at the time on her phone. She was amazed to see she had been asleep for two hours. At least that was a big chunk of the drive done already. Thea got out of the car and followed her mum into the shop whilst her dad topped up their fuel.

"Tee, you can choose a few things for lunch. I know it is a bit early but we won't be stopping until we get to Grandma Maisy's now."

Thea looked around the shop, not really sure on what she fancied. She settled on a cheese sandwich, a chocolate bar and a bottle of lemonade. She handed it all to her mum and thought it best to use the restroom whilst her mum paid. Her mum and dad were already back in the car by the time she was done, although dad was now in the driving seat, and mum was already positioning a pillow under her head. Thea buckled up and immediately sent a picture of the sandwich and chocolate bar to Sarah, hoping she would remember the joke they shared. Within seconds, Sarah had replied.

Hang on! We don't even live together yet!

Yet? Thea held on to that feeling of hope, that one day she would be living with Sarah in a posh penthouse in London. "Off we go again. We might actually get over 50 miles an hour now." he chuckled, looking back at Thea and winking. Her mum didn't even bother to acknowledge what he had said, and continued adjusting her pillow and finally closed her eyes.

Thea was feeling peckish already and decided to eat the cheese sandwich and leave the chocolate bar for later, but once the sandwich had gone, the chocolate bar was looking tastier than ever. That also disappeared rather quickly. She sipped her lemonade, and glanced out the car window. No tall buildings in sight. No pretty city lights. It was green, and turning greener by the mile.

Thea's mum slept for the rest of the drive, but the remaining hours went by rather quickly. Thea and her dad played I Spy, twenty questions and word association games. Her dad had attempted to sing 100 of bottles of beer on the wall, but thankfully gave up when he got to eighty eight. They pulled off the motorway and ended up on some very narrow country roads. They were getting close.

Thea spotted the sign for "Thornton Le Dale" way before the car even got to it. This was it, the new life, the lonely life.

Chapter 3

Grandma Maisy was already in the front garden when they arrived at the house. She was so busy pulling out weeds from the garden path, that she didn't even notice that Thea and her parents had arrived. Thea scrambled out the car first and ran over to her Grandma.

"Grandma Maisy!" she cried out, making her grandma jump slightly.

"Gosh Theadora, you startled me." Grandma Maisy clasped hold of the small picket fence beside her, and used it to help assist her back on to her feet. Thea had never seen her Grandma struggle to get up before.

"Where is my daughter and handsome son in law?" Grandma Maisy questioned, looking around. Thea's mum and dad were already unloading some boxes from the boot of the car.

"For heaven's sake, you have been in the car for hours. Come and have a cup of tea before you start all that." Grandma Maisy gestured all three of them into the house.

Thea took off her jacket and shoes, and clambered on to her favourite arm chair in her Grandma's house, and covered her legs with a blanket. For a summer day, it was still quite chilly. Thea's dad continued to go back and forth to the car, bringing in all the boxes they had bought along with them.

"Sue, the movers called about half an hour ago, they have broken down on the motorway and said not to expect them for at least another 4 to 5 hours." Grandma Maisy winked at Thea, but her mum caught her.

"Mum, please don't joke about these things, you'll be tempting fate."

Grandma Maisy tutted. "Stop worrying and sit down. I will go make some tea. Orange juice Theadora?"

"Yes please." Thea watched Grandma Maisy as she walked into the kitchen. Maisy could still see her through the doorway. Thea had only seen Grandma Maisy at Christmas, but she seemed much more frail than before. Her once dark hair was rippled with white, and her hands seemed a little shaky. Her hand seemed to shake even more as she picked up the kettle and attempted to pour water into the mugs, spilling quite a bit on the worktop. Thea glanced out the front room window and saw her dad was on the phone.

"Sue!" he shouted from the car. "The movers will be here in half an hour!" Grandma Maisy chuckled from the kitchen.

"See Sue, a little joke never hurt anyone."

"Anything can happen in half an hour Mum, anyway, how is dad's old allotment doing?"

"Well, it is all looking a bit shabby in all honesty. It takes a lot of work and I can't bend down for very long now. The other day it took me over ten minutes to get back on my feet. At one point I thought I might have to spend all night there." Thea's mum looked a little concerned.

"Well mum, Thea will help you. She will need something to keep her busy over the summer."

Thea gave her mum a sharp look. She did not want to spend her summer holidays gardening or getting dirty. In fact she couldn't think of anything worse.

"Oh would you, Theadora?" Grandma Maisy asked, looking hopeful.

Thea gave her mum another intense stare.

"Yes Grandma, I would love to help."

"Perfect. Theadora would you mind popping to the shop and getting us some milk? I have just used the last of what I have for these teas."

Thea had got nice and comfy on the arm chair, and actually felt like she could go back to sleep. She realised her mum was staring at her again.

"Yes, no problem Grandma."

She folded up the blanket and went and put her shoes and jacket back on. Grandma Maisy pointed to a five pound note next to the telephone.

"Use that Theadora and grab yourself some sweeties."

Grandma Maisy often spoke to Thea as if she was still a little girl, but she would never actually turn down the chance to get herself some sweets.

Thea got as far as the car and realised her dad was still stood by it.

"Grandma Maisy does actually like you, you know dad. I reckon she will let you inside the house."

Her dad laughed and gave her a little nudge.

"Ha ha very funny Tee. The movers did not sound very certain when I gave them directions to the house, so I am already expecting to have to walk up the road and find them, might as well wait here. Where are you off to so soon?"

"Grandma Maisy has asked me to get her some milk from the shop" she paused to get the five pound note out of her pocket. "Oh, and some sweeties!" she cheered, waving the note in the air.

"Oh, being spoiled already hey?"

"Yep" she replied, looking pleased with herself. She set off on her walk to the shop.

It was only a five minute walk, but her legs still felt quite wobbly from where she had been sitting in the car for so long. The shop was only small and was the only shop in the village. Any big supermarkets were at least a twenty minute drive away. It was quite an old fashioned shop and most of the produce was provided by the local farms. She grabbed a pint of milk and a big bag of pick and mix sweets for herself. George, who owned the shop, stood at the till, counting out some change. He looked up and smiled as soon as he saw Thea.

"Well hello there young Theadora. Have you just arrived? Your Grandma has been so looking forward to today."

Thea liked George a lot. He was a sweet old man and had been a very good friend to her Grandpa when he was alive.

"Hi George, we only arrived half an hour ago and I'm already being sent out on errands."

"Not always a bad thing I guess." he replied, waving the pick and mix in the air.

Thea handed George the five pound note.

"Oh sorry Theadora, I just need to go and get some more one pound coins. Please hang on a moment."

"No problem."

Whilst Thea stood patiently waiting, another young girl walked into the shop.

She had beautiful long blonde hair, all neatly tied up in two french braids. Her skin was even paler than Thea's, something Thea did not think was possible. She wore light denim dungarees over a neon green t-shirt and on her feet she wore some very pretty white Dr Martens boots, that had hand painted bright red roses on. Thea could not take her eyes off her. The young girl turned around and saw Thea staring at her.

"Hello" she said, waving at Thea.

George was suddenly back behind the till.

"Here you go Theadora, sorry, I was struggling to open up the bag."

The young girl stood beside Thea and put a bottle of cola on the counter.

"Theadora, is that your name?" she asked, smiling.

"Well, um, it depends really, well, my Grandma calls me Theadora, my teachers called me Thea and well, um my parents call me Tee." she stuttered. Why did she feel so nervous? She was not one to get shy around new people.

"Rachel, yes this is Theadora." George interrupted "She has just moved to the village with her parents."

"Oh, goodie! Another girl! This village is filled with boys and quite honestly, they are all seriously annoying."

Thea laughed, still feeling a little nervous and took her change from the counter.

"Well I better get home, it was nice to see you George and, um, nice to meet you Rachel."

She shuffled out of the shop rather quickly, wondering why she had felt so starstruck by this girl.

She continued to walk back to Grandma Maisy's house, wait, her house. She needed to get used to that.

Chapter 4

As Thea got closer to home, she could see the moving van parked up behind their car. The van didn't actually carry much more than the beds and some boxes, as Grandma Maisy's house was already furnished. Her parents had to sell most of their furniture from the old house. Luckily for them, Grandma Maisy had her house redecorated a couple of years ago, all very modern and stylish. The decor did not look like an elderly lady lived there at all.

Thea's new room was painted a lovely shade of teal, and had a stunning, large bay window. That was definitely going to be Thea's painting spot. Grandma Maisy had told Thea she could paint the room whatever colour she wanted, but Thea loved the colour already.

Thea put the milk into the fridge and glanced out the kitchen window. She could see her mum and Grandma Maisy were up the top of the garden, looking at Grandpa's allotment.

Thea continued up the stairs to her new room, sweets in hand. She opened her bedroom door to find her dad crouched on the floor, Thea's bed frame was in pieces all over the carpet.

"Oh, dad, you can do your bed first, I don't mind just sleeping on my mattress tonight."

"That was actually the plan Tee, but the movers are currently trying to find the bag of nuts and bolts for it." He rolled his eyes. "The professionals" he said sarcastically.

"Ah, well maybe a sweet would help?" She opened the pick and mix and held out the bag to her dad. He chose a bright red gummy bear.

"Thanks Tee, never too old for sweeties."

"Well do you need help with anything?" Thea asked, hoping he would actually say no. Before he could answer, someone shouted "excuse me" from downstairs.

"Oh hang on Tee, the movers must be finished."

Thea remained at the top of the stairs whilst her dad signed some paperwork and was handed the missing bag of nuts and bolts. The hallway was now filled with boxes, Thea's easel and two mattresses. Thea's dad spoke to her from the bottom of the stairs.

"Why don't you go and see what mum and Grandma are up to? I can sort everything up there. I'll bring your boxes up and you can sort through them later or tomorrow."

Thea made her way back downstairs and put her sweets into the rucksack and got her phone out. She had a message from Sarah.

Have you arrived safely Tee? How was the rest of the trip? Has your mum been really stressed out? How is your new room? x

Thea laughed at the message. She wanted to reply, *Anymore questions?*, but thought it sounded a little rude.

Hi Sar, all three of us and all our stuff have arrived safely. The drive was fine, mum is always stressed out and I have been banished from my room by my dad until he has put the bed up. Miss you x

Thea could see her mum and Grandma Maisy were still in the garden. She trudged up the garden path to the allotment.

"Oh Theadora, thank you for doing that, did you see George?"

"It's okay Grandma. Yes, I saw George. I also met a girl called Rachel." Thea suddenly felt all flushed just mentioning her name. Why did she feel like this?

"Oh Rachel and her family only moved into the village a few months ago. Poor girl."

The doorbell rang and Grandma Maisy started shuffling down the garden path to see who it was.

"Don't worry mum", Thea's mum insisted. "I'll go get that." She began power walking towards the house, but Grandma Maisy carried on shuffling down the garden path. What did Grandma mean? *Poor girl*? Thea stood for a while, pondering on what her Grandma had said. *Poor girl*. Maybe her family weren't very nice or maybe she had been pulled away from her friends and beloved home just like Thea had. Her mum called to her from the kitchen door.

"Thea, there is a girl at the door asking to see you."

Thea looked a tad confused then realised it must be Rachel. She felt a sudden urge to run to the front door, but realised that might look a bit strange, as she had only actually ever spoken one sentence to this girl.

"She has lovely brown curly hair." her mum whispered.

Brown? Well Rachel had long blonde hair, so who was asking for her at the door? Thea walked past her Grandma who was on the phone in the front room, and headed towards the front door, with no actual idea who was there waiting for her.

When she approached the front door, Thea noticed the rose painted white Dr Martens straight away. Her eyes continued up the body, spotting the same denim dungarees and neon top Rachel was wearing earlier, but her mum was not wrong. This girl had bouncy dark brown curly hair. It was Rachel.

"Hi Rachel." Thea tried to smile and not show she was totally confused by the fact Rachel had long blonde hair only thirty minutes ago.

"Hi Theadora, Thea, Tee!"

Thea blushed. "Tee is fine."

"Do you need to help your parents unpack or are you allowed to come out and explore with me? I have been here a few months now, but haven't really made any friends."

Thea couldn't believe she might have just made a friend within an hour of being here. She had accepted this morning before they left, that she would be a loner until she started school. She was also impressed by Rachel's courage to just come and knock on Thea's door after they had barely spoken before.

Thea's mum appeared behind Thea at the door.

"Of course she can go out!" She looked directly at Thea.

"Your dad and I can sort the unpacking. Don't worry we will leave your bits and bobs alone, you can sort that tomorrow."

Thea was happy to be getting out of the house, but was still staring at Rachel's hair whilst her mum spoke.

"Okay, let me just get my jacket and my rucksack." Thea disappeared back into the house for a moment and reappeared with her rucksack on her back and her jacket tied around her waist.

"Cool! Lets go!" Rachel shouted rather loudly, then she skipped down the garden path, gesturing for Thea to follow.

"Bye mum, I will be back later." Her mum smiled, looking pleased for Thea.

Thea had to run to catch up with Rachel. Rachel was a lot taller than Thea and had exceptionally long legs.

"How old are you Rachel?" Thea asked when she finally caught up.

"I am 15, how about you?"

"I will be 15 in a few weeks."

"Oh nice! What are you getting for your birthday?"

"Well I have asked my parents for some new paints, but my mum thinks I need some dresses and makeup to look more like a girl."

"What? Mum's are crazy, you look great just how you are." Thea felt herself blushing again and tried to look away so Rachel could not see.

"Rachel, I hope you don't think I am being rude, but wasn't your hair blonde when I saw you earlier?" Thea wasn't sure if she should ask, but she could not ignore the fact a sudden change in Rachel's appearance had happened so rapidly.

"Oh, yes it was." Rachel smirked. "I wanted to change my hair, but my mum wouldn't let me dye it, so instead she bought me a load of wigs. I had a bright pink bob yesterday." Thea looked shocked at the bright pink bob comment. Rachel saw Thea's face and laughed.

"I am not even joking, my pink wig is my favourite."

"What is your natural hair colour?" Thea replied.

"Boring brown. You have beautiful hair Thea. I have not been brave enough to wear a black wig. My skin looks pale enough as it is."

Their conversation was abruptly interrupted by Rachel's mobile, which was ringing.

"Hi Mum, oh I am really sorry, I forgot. I had just popped out to see Thea, she is the new girl in the village. I will come back home now." Rachel hung up and looked annoyed.

"I am sorry Tee, I need to get back home. How annoying, we have only been out of the house for ten minutes!"

"Is everything okay?"

"Yes, yes, I completely forgot I have a dentist appointment this afternoon."

She held Thea's hand and Thea's heart felt like it was going to burst right out of her chest.

"I will come and fetch you tomorrow instead, how does that sound?"

Inside, Thea wanted to scream YES! But she knew that would make things super awkward.

"That sounds good to me, anytime will be fine."

Rachel let go of Thea's hand and started to walk away.

"See you tomorrow Tee!"

Thea stood watching Rachel walk away, until she disappeared around the corner.

She was already looking forward to tomorrow.

Chapter 5

When Thea arrived back home, her mum and dad were struggling up the stairs with her mattress.

"Oh, back already Tee?" her mum asked.

"Sue, can you please engage in a conversation once we have got this to Tee's room please? This is killing my back!"

"Yes, sorry, two seconds Tee".

Thea stood and ate some of her sweets whilst they shifted the mattress up the stairs.

"Dinner and a show ey?" Grandma Maisy said, appearing from the Kitchen and taking a couple of Thea's sweets.

"Yes, don't worry you two down there. Just keep watching us wrestle with this thing", her dad muttered.

"Oh we intend to," Grandma Maisy replied, giving Thea a little nudge.

"Right you can come up Tee and sort your bedding out" her mum chirped. "All your boxes and bags of clothes are up here too. You can arrange it to how you want it all and there is a bag of clothes hangers in the wardrobe."

"I guess that is my afternoon planned out then" Thea groaned, looking at Grandma Maisy.

"Best to get it all sorted anyway Theadora, don't drag it out."

"Don't forget to grab your easel." her mum shouted from Thea's bedroom.

Thea lugged the easel up the stairs, and found her mum was sorting her bedding for her anyway.

"Right, bed one done, on to bed two" her dad grumbled, and he made for their bedroom.

"So why are you back so soon, Tee?" her mum questioned, plumping Thea's pillows.

"Rachel forgot she had a dentist appointment, she had to get home."

"Oh that's a shame, she's very tall isn't she? Is she your age?"

"She is already 15 and we are going to go out tomorrow instead, if you don't have anything planned for me?"

"No, you go out, play, do whatever."

"15 year old's don't *play* mum, they just *hang*."

"Well whatever it is you do, just don't get into trouble."

Thea looked at her mum, astounded and what she had just said.

"Mum, I have never got into trouble in my entire life!"

"Well then, don't start now, will you. Right, bedding sorted. Your duvet cover goes nicely with the walls already, look at that."

"Yeah, it looks nice mum. I've got it from here thanks."

"No problem, I will call you when dinner is ready."

Thea's mum left the room leaving Thea stood in the middle of boxes and bags of clothes. Thea sat on the end of her bed and checked her phone. One message from Sarah.

I am glad you got there safe, Tee. We have to leave at 2am tomorrow morning for our flight. Mum doesn't want me to take my phone because of how much it costs to use it abroad. Don't miss me too much! Xx

Thea had forgotten Sarah and her family were going on holiday. She would be in France for two weeks and was uncontactable by the sounds of it. Thea lay back on her bed and immediately her thoughts turned to Rachel. She suddenly felt a little flushed again. Why did her heart feel like it was going to explode when Rachel held her hand earlier? Sarah had held her hand a million times, but she had never felt like that. Thea began to imagine Sarah and what she looked like. Sarah was a slim girl, only slightly taller than Thea, and she had short, curly red hair. She imagined the freckles all over Sarah's face, and her bright purple glasses that often slipped down her nose. Thea had always thought Sarah was a sweet looking girl, but she didn't find her *attractive*.

She switched her mind back to Rachel. She preferred her with the blonde french braids over the brown wavy hair, but she looked nice with either. Her mind shot back to the hand hold again, and her heart started racing. She sat up swiftly. She had never really been into boys, not yet anyway, but surely that didn't mean she was into girls? Was she?

"Do I *fancy* Rachel?" she whispered to herself. She felt weird saying it, but her mind was not shutting down the fact this could be what was happening. She realised, since moving to the village, she had only spent a total of about twenty minutes with Rachel. She couldn't decide if she fancied someone after only twenty minutes. This feeling she had could just be a strong feeling of admiration towards Rachel. She would see how she felt tomorrow.

She got her phone and thought she better reply to Sarah. She decided not to mention making a new friend, as it might sound like she had replaced Sarah already.

"2am? I wouldn't bother going to bed! But I know you like your sleep. Have a great holiday and you know I will miss you too much xx

Thea started to hang up all her clothes, although she was tempted to just chuck all the bags into the wardrobe and take what she wanted from the bags each day. She knew her mum would go crazy if she did that, so continued to hang it all up, very unenthusiastically.

She got through all 4 bags of clothing, and couldn't bear the thought of starting on the boxes yet.

She lay on her bed and stared out the window. All she could see were green fields and some sheep way off in the distance. It was so quiet here. In London she could always hear the busy roads outside, cars honking and the general hustle and bustle of the streets when her bedroom window was open. It felt too quiet here. She closed her eyes and tried to think about what her new school would be like. Her new uniform was green, as if there wasn't enough green around here.

She must have drifted off, because she awoke to Grandma Maisy stroking her hair softly.

"Hey there sleepy head. Dinner is ready."

Thea slowly opened her eyes.

"Okay, Grandma, I will be down in a minute."

"No worries, but don't take too long, your dad will eat all the chow mein."

Thea shot up. "You got chinese takeaway?" she shrieked with excitement.

"Well, we have to make the first night here special. Come on, let's eat."

Thea and Grandma Maisy headed towards the stairs,

"Go down before me, Theadora, it takes me a little while now."

Thea looked saddened at her Grandma's words. She led the way down the stairs, and sat down at the dining table next to her mum.

"Nice little snooze, Tee?" her mum asked. "It has been a tiring day hasn't it?"

"I didn't mean to fall asleep." Thea was already spooning rice and chow mein on to her plate. Grandma Maisy placed a can of cola next to Thea's plate.

"Thank you Grandma."

"You are most welcome." Grandma Maisy sat down next to Thea's dad. "So how did Rachel seem today, Thea?"

"She was really nice, Grandma. I didn't get to see her for very long, she had an appointment to get to".

"Ah, another hospital appointment I can only imagine." Grandma shook her head with a sympathetic look on her face.

"Well, she said it was the dentist. Why did you assume it was a hospital appointment Grandma?"

Grandma Maisy obviously knew something Thea did not.

"Rachel is not very well, Theadora."

"I did think she looked a bit pale when she was at the door earlier" her mum chimed in.

"What do you mean she isn't very well Grandma?" Thea had stopped spooning food on to her plate and was feeling anxious, not really sure she wanted Grandma Maisy to answer.

"Well sweetheart, she has cancer, of the pelvis if I remember rightly."

Thea suddenly did not feel hungry at all. Cancer? Rachel didn't look like someone that had cancer, but then Thea realised she had no idea what someone with cancer looked like.

Thea immediately thought about Rachel's unexpected hair change earlier, the wigs. It all made sense now.

"Are you okay, Tee?" Her dad must have seen the muddled look on Thea's face.

"I think so. I just can't believe what Grandma just said. Are the treatments working Grandma?"

"I don't really know much about it I'm afraid, but she looks much better than she did when she first moved into the village."

Thea tried to eat as much as she could, but the food just wasn't tasting right. She sat thinking to herself whilst her parents had moved on to the subject of their new jobs.

Was Rachel really that ill? Grandma maisy had said she was looking much better than before, so the treatments must be working. Rachel was bouncy and energetic earlier, not tired or ill looking.

Thea's dad noticed Thea staring at her plate, not eating anything. He squeezed her hand.

"Would you like to take your dinner to your room, Tee?"

Thea had never been offered to take her dinner to her room before, her mum would never let her. She noticed her dad was glancing over at her mum.

"Actually Tee, why don't you?"

Thea realised her parents had obviously noticed that the news about Rachel had got to her.

"If you don't mind, that would be great." Thea replied. "I think I will go to bed after I have eaten, I will bring my plate down in the morning. Night everyone."

"Goodnight" all three of them chorused.

Thea took her plate and her can of drink up to her room, but placed the plate of food straight on the floor. She sat on her bed, her mind was buzzing like crazy. She wouldn't have expected Rachel to tell her she had cancer, when they hadn't properly spoken to each other yet, but maybe she was going to? Thea was more worried than excited about tomorrow now. What if she started acting weird around Rachel, now knowing what she knows? Thea got into her pyjamas, went and brushed her teeth and stumbled back to bed. She lay there awake for what seemed like hours.

Chapter 6

Thea was already standing by her wardrobe, trying to choose an outfit, when her alarm went off. She wanted to look nice, not like she was trying too hard, but her normal baggy attire was not going to cut it today. The sun was already shining and she had heard her mum telling Grandma Maisy it was going to be hot today.

She grabbed hold of some black denim shorts and held them up against her, whilst looking in her mirror. She had always thought they were too short, anything above the knee was always too much for her, but her mum had always said they looked nice. Right, bottoms sorted, now what top to wear? She fished through all the clothes hanging in front of her. All she could find were lots of baggy t-shirts and jumpers. She put on a white oversized t-shirt and put a thin black belt around her waist. She was impressed with her fashion improvisation, she had never really bothered to try before. She finished the look with a bright red pair of converse, put her hair into the normal messy bun and skipped down the stairs.

"Wow, now that's an outfit, Tee!" her mum marvelled, grabbing Thea's arm and making her do a spin.

"Stop it, mum!"

"I love it! But you could have done something with your hair…"

"Mum!"

"Alright, alright. What time is Rachel coming by anyway?"

"Well, actually...I don't know." Thea remembered no time had properly been agreed, Rachel just said she would be over at some point.

"I am sure I have time for some toast though." She looked hopefully at her mum who was spreading jam over her own piece of toast. Her mum sighed.

"Fine, have this piece, I will make myself some more I suppose."

"Thanks, mum" Thea smiled, taking the plate from her mum. As soon as she took the plate, she realised her dinner from the night before was still on her bedroom floor. Her mum hadn't mentioned it, so she kept quiet.

"So how are you feeling today anyway? I know what Grandma told you last night had upset you."

"I am trying not to think about it really. I am obviously not going to ask Rachel about it. I will wait to see if she would like to tell me herself."

"That is a good idea, Tee. Rachel seemed very upbeat and lively yesterday, maybe she is in recovery." Thea was hoping that was the case.

Thea was just finishing her toast when there was a loud knock at the door. Dad got there first.

"Tee! Rachel is at the door." Another weird wave of emotion washed Tee, she was frozen.

"Tee! Did you hear me?" her dad bellowed down the hallway.

"Come on Tee, don't keep her waiting." Her mum ushered her out the kitchen and towards the front door. Thea wondered what hair Rachel would have today. The brown wavy hair was back, no pink bob. Rachel was wearing a beautiful black floaty summer dress that was embroidered with red roses. It matched her rose painted Dr Martens perfectly.

"Morning, Tee!" she greeted, "Oh, cool outfit!"

Thea loved that Rachel had already complimented her. Thea put her phone in her pocket and shouted goodbye to her parents.

"Shall we go for a walk down by the lake, Tee?"

"Okay. So, I was half expecting the pink bob today."

"Well, I was thinking about it, but then I thought it best to stick with the same hair around your parents to stop them getting confused!"

"That makes sense I guess. How was your dentist appointment?"

"My teeth are perfect, as always." She grinned at Thea, showing all her bright white teeth. Thea had no reason to believe Rachel had lied to her, it might really have been a dentist appointment.

"You have a lovely smile Rachel." Thea instantly cringed. Why did she just say that?

"Thanks, Tee. You can never smile enough." Thea sighed with relief. She seemed to have gotten away with that one.

"Do you go to Saint Peter's upper school? I am starting there next term."

"No, I don't go to school anymore, my mum home schools me. That is why I haven't made any friends here yet."

"Can't you ask to go to a school?" Thea didn't know anyone that was home schooled. She couldn't imagine her mum trying to teach her anything, she gets annoyed enough if Thea asks her for help with her homework.

"I don't mind it really. It is quite nice spending time with my mum and I don't have to wear a horrible uniform."

"I will soon be wearing that *horrible uniform*, thank you very much!"

They both laughed. Thea found it so easy to talk to Rachel, it was like they had known each other for years.

"Shall we go to the shop first, Tee? We could grab a drink to take down to the lake. It is really warm today."

"I didn't bring any money, Thea said, looking slightly embarrassed.

"My treat." Rachel insisted, heading towards the shop.

Rachel had suggested they get a drink, but she started picking allsorts from the shelves. Rachel grabbed two bottles of cola, checking with Thea first that she was happy with cola, a share bag of cheesy crisps, some cocktail sausages and a huge chocolate bar.

"A great day for a picnic ey ladies?" George chirped as Rachel put all the goodies on the counter.

"It sure is George" Rachel replied. "Can we have a bag please?"

"Of course." George put everything in a bag and Rachel handed over a ten pound note.

I wish my parents would give me £10 Thea thought to herself. George handed Rachel her change.

"Have a lovely time ladies". George waved as they left the shop.

"You didn't have to get all that Rachel, I feel bad."

"Don't be silly, Tee. I am allowed to treat my friend aren't I?"

My friend. Rachel said *my friend.* Thea felt all tingly inside. The walk to the lake from the shop only took fifteen minutes. Thea and Rachel chatted continuously the whole way . They talked about books, movies, and where they both used to live. Thea found out that Rachel had moved from Cornwall, and that she really missed the beach. The sun seemed to be getting even hotter, so they seated themselves on a bench in the shade right next to the lake. Rachel handed Thea her drink, opened all the food and placed it all on the bench between them.

"Go ahead, Tee, or I will eat it all."

Thea helped herself to some crisps. She noticed Rachel was fidgeting quite a lot.

"Have you got ants in your pants?" Thea giggled.

"No! Gross! I get achy bones sometimes, nothing major."

Thea had forgotten about Rachel's illness up to this point, and now she had no idea what to say.

"Oh do you? Why's that?" Thea couldnt't help but ask, maybe Rachel would open up to her about it all.

"Creaky bones! Run's in the family, although I might just take some painkillers, it can help."

Rachel unzipped the little pocket on her dress and pulled out a packet of tablets. Thea did not recognise the box, it wasn't like any painkillers she had taken before. Rachel knocked a couple of them back, using the cola to wash them down.

"That should do the trick!"

Thea looked down at her feet.

"Are you okay, Tee?"

"Yep, just feeling quite warm, even in the shade."

"It is really hot today, we better eat this chocolate quickly, or we will end up with chocolate soup!"

Rachel snapped the chocolate bar and handed half to Thea. It was already starting to melt and both of them ended up with chocolate all over their hands. They ate it all as quickly as they could, but the chocolate stains on their hands remained.

"Rachel, come down to this bank. We can wash it off in the lake. My dad always made me do this when I was little. I fell over in the mud alot."

"That is cute, I can imagine a tiny little Tee plodding along, then falling face first into the mud."

"Ha ha, very funny! Now get down here and wash off your hands."

Rachel knelt down next to Thea, but she noticed Rachel made a face as she crouched down, like she was in pain.

"Are you sure you are okay Rachel?" Thea asked, looking concerned.

Rachel looked Thea straight in the eyes. She looked for a good five seconds.

"What?" Thea questioned.

"You know, don't you?"

Thea gulped. She felt even hotter than before.

"Know what?"

"Who has been blabbing?" Rachel did not look annoyed, it was more of an unsettled look.

Thea sat back on the grass. Rachel was still giving her an intense stare.

"Last night at dinner, my Grandma said that you were not very well. That's all."

Rachel sighed deeply and sat back on the bench.

"I am okay, Tee, see? I mean, I walked here didn't I?"

"You did, but you don't have to hide anything from me."

"I wasn't trying to hide anything from you. I just don't often meet new people and say *Hi I'm Rachel and I have cancer.*"

The way Rachel blurted that sentence out made Thea feel uneasy.

"Sorry, that was not meant to come across rude." Rachel apologised.

"Don't worry about it. I won't ask anymore questions, deal?"

"Deal." Rachel smiled and put her hand out to shake Thea's.

"Wash that chocolate off first please!"

The rest of the afternoon was perfect. Thea showed Rachel the rope swing in the woods that her dad used to take her to. Rachel looked amazing, glowing in the rays of sunlight that were shining through the trees, her dress flowing as she swung back and forth. Thea decided she liked Rachel. She liked Rachel a lot.

Chapter 7

The hours seemed to go by so fast, and Rachel's phone began to ring as it hit five o clock.

"Hi Mum, no problem, I will make my way back now, love you."

"Dinner time?" Thea asked.

"Yes, already! How did that happen?"

Rachel's house was in the opposite direction to Thea's from the lake.

"Well I best go off this way and you best go off that way" Rachel joked, doing a little dance pointing in all directions.

"You are odd!" Thea mocked. "Well, are you busy tomorrow?" Thea asked, hoping she could see Rachel every day for the rest of the summer holidays.

"I have an appointment quite early tomorrow morning."

Thea looked away, not sure what to say.

"Don't worry Tee, it is just a check up, things have been going really well." Rachel smiled and stepped closer to Thea. "I will come and get you when I am back, if you want to go out again?"

"I would love to!" Thea realised she blurted that out like an excited child, but Rachel never seemed to notice or care how over enthusiastic she was.

"Fabulous. I will probably be back just after lunch, the check ups can take a while. Thanks for a great day Tee."

Rachel moved even closer to Thea and pulled her in for a hug. The world seemed to spin faster and faster around them. Rachel smelt so sweet and her skin felt so soft. Thea hoped the hug would never end, but of course, it did. Rachel took their bag of rubbish and began to bounce across the field towards her house.

"Until tomorrow, Tee!"

"Bye Rachel, I can't wait!"

Thea headed home, her heart still thumping from the hug. She thought about Rachel's appointment tomorrow, just a check up, that sounded good. When she walked through the front door, she could smell something amazing, then she realised. Grandma Maisy could make the most delicious pizzas from scratch and that was definitely what the smell was coming from the kitchen. Her mum appeared in the hallway.

"Would you look at that for timing, I was just about to call you. Pizzas will be ready in about ten minutes."

"Awesome, it smells so good. I am just going to go and wash my hands and get changed."

Thea was quite happy with her outfit of choice today, but she couldn't wait to get back into her lounge about cosy clothes. She went up to her bedroom and changed into some tracksuit bottoms and a long sleeved loose fitted top. That was better. She went to put her t-shirt into the wash basket, and smelt something sweet as she picked it up. It smelt like Rachel. Some of Rachel's perfume must have rubbed off on it during the hug. Thea clasped the sweet smelling t-shirt close to her chest and breathed deeply. There was definitely no denying it after today, she fancied Rachel. Her head began to spin, so much so, she needed to hold on to her wardrobe door to steady herself. She still wasn't certain if she only liked girls, but she undoubtedly liked Rachel. Thea got butterflies everytime she thought about her. She pictured Rachel sat on the rope swing, smiling, laughing. Thea felt dizzy again.

"Tee! Pizza time!" her mum shouted up the stairs.

"I'll just be one minute." she replied.

Thea went into the bathroom and washed her hands, as lake water probably wasn't the cleanest. She patted a cold flannel across her face, she seemed to be blushing again, a lot.

She made her way downstairs, the pizza smelt incredible.

"Did you have a good day, Theadora?" Grandma Maisy asked.

"It was really good thank you. Rachel bought us some picnic food and I showed her the rope swing dad used to take me to."

Her dad strolled into the dining room, holding two pizzas.

"That swing is still there? Be careful of that, who knows how much that rope has decayed over the years." He placed a pizza in front of Thea.

"Well, it took Rachel's weight okay."

"She is only small I suppose." her mum replied "Tall, but very slim."

"She has a check up appointment tomorrow." Thea explained, "she said things have been going well."

Her dad smiled at her.

"Well that is great news, Tee. I am glad you have made such a nice friend already."

"Thanks dad, she is really great." Thea couldn't stop smiling and the pizza was making her feel even more content. Thea scoffed down her pizza in less than ten minutes and even managed the last slice of her mum's.

"You do amaze me, Tee *and* you stay so small" her mum teased.

"That pizza was amazing as always Grandma, thank you. Can I go to my room, mum? I still have a couple of boxes to sort."

"Of course, and please remember to bring down last night's plate at some point?" She winked at Tee.

"Oh yeah....sorry mum."

Thea wasn't planning on sorting the last boxes in her room at all. She wanted to paint and she knew exactly who she wanted to paint. She checked her phone. No message from Sarah of course. She really wanted to be able to message Rachel, she must remember to ask for her number tomorrow. She routed through one of her boxes and found a small square plain canvas. She hunted for a pencil in her rucksack and began sketching the outline of Rachel's body on the swing. Once she had the rough outline sorted, she fetched her paints and began to create her portrait. She chose a vivid crimson for the roses on Rachels dress and boots. Thea decided to paint Rachel with her long blonde braids, and made sure to capture her beautiful smile.

The summer sun had disappeared by the time she had finished and the moon was shining brighter than ever. Thea looked out at the clear sky, millions of stars sparkled up above, a view she was not used to in London. She had been so upset about moving here, but so far it was going pretty well. She glanced back at her painting of Rachel and sighed. Would she ever be able to tell Rachel how she felt? Rachel probably had enough going on in her life, with the cancer, how would she feel if a girl she met two days ago told her she fancied her?

Thea decided for now, it would be best to keep it to herself.

She heard a light tap on her door, and Grandma Maisy stepped into her bedroom.

"'We are all off to bed, Tee, what have you been up to?"

Thea suddenly felt embarrassed by her painting and turned her easel away so Grandma Maisy couldn't see.

"I am not happy with this one yet, Grandma. You can see it when I have sorted it."

"Always a perfectionist, like your mother. It is getting late though, don't stay up too much longer, will you?"

"I won't, night Grandma."

Grandma Maisy left the room, leaving Thea to stare at her artwork. She had thought about giving the canvas to Rachel as a present, but maybe it was too soon. She would wait a bit on that one too.

Thea couldn't be bothered to change into her pyjamas, she got into bed wearing her cosy lounging clothes, they were basically the same thing anyway. She closed her eyes and thought about Sarah. Would she even tell Sarah what was going on in her head, when she returned from France? She was struggling to process her own feelings without having to worry about telling anyone else. She wondered what her parents would think. Her mum and dad had always been very understanding and were easy to talk to, but this was on a whole other level. She shuffled down right under the duvet and grunted loudly to herself. Whoever said being a teenager was fun, lied.

Chapter 8

Thea woke to a loud banging noise coming from the garden. She got up and looked out her window. Her dad was in the allotment, hammering wooden stakes into the ground. It was only nine o clock, Rachel wouldn't be over for a few hours yet. She got dressed and made her way to the garden.

"Do you need any help dad?" she asked, reluctantly.

"You must be bored, Tee, you hate dirt."

"Yes, well I'm pretty much unpacked, it is nice weather and Rachel won't be over until after lunch, so…"

"I would appreciate the help. Your mum and Grandma have gone to the market so they probably won't reappear for a good couple of hours."

"What are we going to try and grow this year?"

"Not too sure yet, your Grandma is picking up all the seeds at the market. We need to pull out all the weeds and level out the dirt first."

Thea realised she really did not want to do this, but her dad seemed to be enjoying her company.

"So, you and Rachel seem to be getting on well?"

"Yeah, she is really nice and fun to be around."

"That is great to hear, Tee. Does she go to St Peters?"

"No, she is home schooled by her mum. I did wonder why at first, as she told me before I knew she was unwell, but maybe it has been easier to teach her at home."

"Very true. Well maybe, if her treatment is going well, she may be able to start school again."

Thea thought about what her dad just said. She would *love* it if Rachel went to her school, she would be able to see her everyday.

"That would be great if she could, then I would already have a friend at St Peters."

"Fingers crossed then ey? Right, grab some gardening gloves from the shed, we can start on the weeds."

Thea had not been in the shed since her Grandpa had passed away, but it still smelt like cigars. There was a chair in the corner where he used to smoke his cigars, even though Grandma Maisy would go mad and tell him he would one day burn down the shed if he wasn't careful. She took some gloves and swiftly left when she noticed all the cobwebs up above her.

"Do you think Grandma Maisy misses Grandpa all the time?" she asked her dad.

"Most definitely. I miss both my parents every day and they died 16 years ago. I wish you got to meet them, Tee, my mum loved to paint and draw. You take after her for sure."

"I wish I had got to meet them too. I know I didn't want to move here at first, but I am glad Grandma Maisy isn't lonely anymore. It must be horrible being on your own all the time."

"Exactly that, Tee. And she has all of us, what more could she want?" He chuckled and winked at Thea.

Thea picked out weeds until her back was sore. She stood up, reached to the sky and stretched loudly.

"You done in, Tee?"

"It feels like I have been bent over for *hours.*"

"Well, look who it is." her dad nodded his head towards the house.

Thea turned around to see her mum and Rachel walking up to the allotment.

"I found a stranger outside!" her mum announced.

"Sorry, I did knock, but I guess you couldn't hear me from all the way up here!" Rachel joked.

"Oh, how embarrassing, sorry Rachel, you should have opened the front door and shouted up." her dad replied.

Thea looked down at herself, covered in dirt, sweating, and looking just genuinely awful. Great, what a look for Rachel too see.

"I have bought back some eggs and bacon to make some nice baguettes for lunch, have you eaten yet Rachel?" her mum asked.

"No, I haven't. Do you mind if I stay for lunch?"

"Course not! I wouldn't have asked otherwise!"

Thea loved that Rachel was staying for lunch, but was more concerned about making herself look more presentable.

"I am just going to go and sort myself out." Thea blurted out. "I will be as quick as possible."

Thea ran down the garden path and to her bedroom. She looked at herself in the mirror.

"Oh my god." she cried out loud. She ran to the bathroom and washed her hands, face and underarms as quickly as she could, splashing water everywhere in the process. Her hair looked like it could do with a wash but there was definitely no time for that. She sprayed it with copious amounts of dry shampoo and styled it into a plait. She put on some black leggings and her favourite baby pink baggy t-shirt. That would have to do.

When she arrived back in the kitchen, Rachel was standing buttering the baguettes.

"Mum!" Thea cried. "You don't ask guests to butter baguettes."

"I offered, Tee! I felt bad watching your mum do all the work." Rachel smiled at Thea, waving the butter knife in the air.

"Oh, well then, carry on." Thea laughed.

"Tee, Grandma has gone to her friends for coffee, can you take your dad's lunch up to him, will be just us girls in here." Thea was actually hoping her mum would leave her and Rachel alone. She took her dad his baguette and returned to find Rachel and her mum talking about Rachel's appointment she had that morning.

"Tee, Rachel has some amazing news!" Her mum said, looking excited.

"I do, I have been told today that I don't need another check up for 6 months."

"Wow, rachel! That is good news! We need to celebrate!". Thea grinned at Rachel, she was so happy for her.

"Would you like Rachel to stay over tonight? A little sleepover to celebrate?".

"Oh! Rachel, would you like to? It would be so fun!". Rachel had just taken a big bite of her baguette.

"I would love to!" she scoffed. "I will call my mum after lunch and ask."

Thea was so excited. First Rachel's good news and she was possibly sleeping over. They all chatted and laughed through lunch, it felt so nice everyone getting along, it was almost like having Sarah in the house.

Rachel went into the hallway to ring her mum, Thea crossed her fingers hoping for a yes.

"Sue, will I need any bedding? Mum doesn't know where my sleeping bag is!" Rachel shouted into the kitchen.

"Tell your mum not to worry, Thea has a double bed, you can both bundle up in there!"

Thea suddenly felt hot. It was only yesterday she realised she fancied Rachel and now she was going to be sharing a bed with her. Rachel came back into the kitchen looking all pleased.

"Well, I better go home and fetch some jim jams! Maybe some sweet treats for a midnight feast." she squealed.

"Are you sure you don't mind sharing my bed, Rachel?"

"Of course not! It will be cosy."

Cosy. That is exactly what Thea was worried about.

"Rachel, do you like spaghetti bolognese? That is the plan for dinner tonight."

"That sounds delicious, thank you. Although, I might swap my white top for a black one."

Thea's mum laughed. "Well, you get home and get your things, we will go put some nice fresh bedding on Thea's bed."

"We only put clean bedding on a couple of days ago!" Thea sighed.

"Yes well, you have a guest."

Rachel headed towards the door.

"See you in a little bit guys!"

Thea couldn't believe this was happening, Rachel was going to be there all night, in her bed. She had still forgotten to get her number though.

Chapter 9

"Mum, I would like to have a shower before I sort the bedding, I won't be long."

Thea was long. She washed her hair thoroughly, scrubbed her body more than she normally would and made sure to shave her legs in case there was any accidental leg touching in the bed. She finished up and made her way to her bedroom and noticed her bedding was already changed.

"Thanks, mum!" she shouted down the stairs.

"I know, I know, you love me!" her mum replied.

Thea sat in front of her mirror, wrapped in her towel. She was delighted that Rachel was staying over, but she was quite nervous. She wondered if her parents would have let Rachel stay in her room, in her bed, if they really knew how she felt about her. Course they wouldn't. It would be the same as her asking if a boy could stay in her bed, wouldn't it?

She dried her hair and tied it back into a plait, but it looked much nicer now her hair was clean. She put on some black skinny jeans and a baggy hoodie. Thea looked nice in anything she wore, not that she knew that herself. She didn't really need to tidy her room, it had hardly been lived in yet, but she noticed the plate of old chinese was gone, another thing to thank her mum for.

She realised she had not seen Grandma Maisy all day, she had better go and find her. She wandered downstairs and saw Grandma Maisy was sitting in the lounge, reading the paper.

"Hi Grandma, have you had a nice day out and about?" Thea asked.

Grandma Maisy peered over the top of her paper.

"Hello Theadora, it has been nice thank you. I met Lily for a coffee, she sends her love."

Lily was married to George who owned the shop and was Grandma Maisy's best friend. Thea always thought her and Sarah would be like Grandma and Lily, they had known each other since they were teenagers.

"I will have to pop over and see her soon, maybe next time you go, I will come with you."

"She would love that, Theadora."

There was a loud knock on the door, Thea's heart skipped a beat. She took a deep breath and answered the door. There it was, the bright pink bob. When Thea had pictured the bob, she imagined it bright neon pink, a bit tacky looking, but it was not like that at all. The wig was a pale pink that was styled with soft short curls, it looked incredible on Rachel.

"Wow, that is some cool looking hair!" Thea marvelled.

"I knew you would love it" Rachel did a little spin, posing as she landed.

"Come in, come in" her mum called from the kitchen.

"Dinner will still be an hour or so yet, so why don't you take Rachel's things up to your room?".

"Come on Rachel, let me carry your bag." Thea took Rachels bag and led her to the bedroom.

"You have a beautiful room Tee, look at that bay window!".

"Thank you, that is my favourite part of the room."

"Oh what have you been painting? Let me go and have a look."

Thea froze. She forgot the canvas was still on the easel. Oh no, Rachel was now going to think Thea was some weird stalker and she would grab her bag and run straight home. She watched Rachel closely as she examined the painting.

There was a moment of silence and Thea noticed a tear rolling down Rachel's cheek. Great, the painting creeped her out so much, she made Rachel cry.

"Tee….this is beautiful, you've made me look beautiful."

Thea sighed an enormous sigh of relief.

"You are beautiful, Rachel! What are the tears for?"

"I just love it so much and the fact you wanted to paint me makes me feel so special."

"You are special to me." Thea blushed.

"Can I have it?" Rachel asked "Or do you like to keep all your artwork? I would understand if that's the case."

Thea couldn't believe this was happening, this was going much better than she expected.

"Of course you can, I would love you to keep it."

Rachel ran up to Thea and gave her an intense hug.

"Thank you, thank you, my talented friend."

Thea hugged her back, not wanting to let go.

"Can you show me some more of your artwork?"

"If you like, let me get my sketchbooks." Thea retrieved 3 large sketchbooks from under her bed. She looked at Rachel and patted the bed, inviting her to sit next to her. Rachel got on to the bed and crossed her legs.

"Okay, let me see!" Rachel demanded.

Rachel went through all the sketchbooks one by one, admiring all of Thea's sketches and paintings. She caressed the pages and continued to complement Thea throughout.

"I wish I was good at something like this." Rachel moaned.

"You are an artist in your own way. You have a great sense of fashion, you always look fantastic!"

That evening, Rachel was wearing some dark grey ripped jeans and a tight white shirt with a silver and black fitted waistcoat over the top. Thea loved the way she dressed.

"Thank you, Tee. I guess fashion is an art in its own way."

"Of course it is, and you really have an eye for it."

Thea's mum knocked on the door.

"Dinner, girls."

Thea was worried about dinner. Parents can be embarrassing at the best of times, but it would be even worse in front of Rachel. Her mum bought their dinner into the dining room, followed by her dad who handed the girls a can of cola each.

"Thank you Sue, thank you Kevin." Rachel beamed.

"I am glad you have made a very polite friend, Tee." her dad nudged Rachel on the arm.

"I am very lucky to have Tee, as a friend!"

Thea could feel herself turning red, this seemed to be happening a lot lately.

"Well, get that dinner down you, I nipped to the shop and got you girls some sweet treats for afters,"

"Thanks, mum! By the way, where is Grandma Maisy?"

"It's bingo night at the village hall, they serve all the players dinner too."

"Those elderlies can get quite aggressive at bingo night!" her dad joked.

Thea and Rachel started to giggle, Rachel pretended to whack Thea with an invisible walking stick.

"Stop that" her mum sniggered. "It is nice that she still gets out of the house anyway".

Thea and Rachel devoured their dinner as fast as they could. They wanted to get back to their sleepover. Thea's mum handed her a bag that contained some more cans of cola, a bag of strawberry laces, chocolate buttons and some giant white chocolate cookies.

"Woah, thanks mum!".

The girls scarpered upstairs to Thea's room and tipped all the treats on to the bed, once Thea had put the sketchbooks away. Rachel went for a giant cookie, whilst Thea sat and tied some strawberry laces into knots and plaits before eating them.

"Oh! Thea, watching you do those plaits has reminded me, I bought some yarns for us to make friendship bracelets!"

Rachel excitedly jumped off the bed and got her bag. She pulled out a box that contained what looked like hundreds of colourful yarns.

"Wow!" Thea stared at the box, all the colours looked amazing.

"Well, we can both choose 3 colours and we will make each others, yeah?"

"Okay, great. I definitely want some kind of pink in mine, and I wear black a lot."

"Right, black, pink and how about a silver glittery one to brighten it up?" Rachel took the 3 colours and held them together so Thea could see what they all looked like.

"You really do have an eye for colours, that will look amazing. Okay now choose yours."

Rachel glanced over all the yarns, picking some up, putting them back, picking more up, until she finally settled on a turquoise blue, a lime green and a bright yellow.

"There, super bright!". Rachel looked pleased with her choices.

The girls sat and concentrated on neatly plaiting the yarns together, Thea thought Rachel's looked beautiful. All the vibrant colours really portrayed Rachel's bright and bubbly personality.

"Give me your arm, Tee, yours is done and it looks *fab-u-lous.*"

Thea placed her hand on Rachel's knee whilst Rachel tied on her bracelet.

"It looks really good, Rachel" Thea said, waving her arm around so that the silver yarn shone in the light.

"Your turn, let's have your arm."

Rachel held out her arm and let Tee tie on her bracelet. Once it was secure, Rachel held Thea's hand so she could see the bracelets next to each other. Thea couldn't stop smiling, it was like they were in their own little world and she never wanted to leave.

"They both look brilliant, don't they, Tee?"

Thea squeezed Rachel's hand tight. "I love them."

"How about we get into our pyjamas? We will be much cosier then."

"Okay, you can go and get changed in the bathroom if you like."

Rachel picked up her bag and walked towards the bedroom door.

"I shall be back in a minute." Rachel smiled.

Thea quickly changed into some baggy pyjama shorts and an even baggier t-shirt. Proper comfy clothes. She couldn't believe it when Rachel came back into the room. Rachel was wearing a pale green silky nighty, trimmed in neon pink lace. It was beautiful, she looked like a movie star.

"Well, your pyjamas look much comfier than mine." Rachel giggled. Thea couldn't take her eyes off her. Rachel put her bag down and got under the duvet, whilst Thea stayed sitting on the end of the bed.

"Come on Thea, I don't take up too much room" Rachel joked.

Thea turned on her bedside lamp and turned off the main bedroom light. She got into bed and started to nibble on a cookie.

"It was nice of your mum to get us all these treats, Tee." She opened the bag of chocolate buttons. "Hopefully we won't get covered in chocolate this time."

"Rachel, do you think you might start school again, if you are getting better?"

Rachel hesitated, "I don't really know what my mum wants me to do yet, but I could always ask her."

"It would be so fun if we went to school together, although we would probably have to hide you from all the boys."

"You make me laugh, I am not really interested in boys."

Thea didn't know how to take what Rachel had just said. Did she mean she liked girls, or liked boys, but wasn't interested in them right now?

"What's wrong with boys?" Thea asked, trying to get more information.

"Nothing, well boys our age are just annoying aren't they. Plus I don't need boys, I have you." She looked at Thea and smiled. Thea was more than satisfied with Rachel's answer.

"Do you mind if I go to sleep Thea? You don't have to, today has just made me very tired and my painkillers can make me feel quite drowsy."

"We can go to sleep if you like, do you want me to turn the lamp off, and then you can take your wig off? Or…"

"Don't look so awkward Tee, I do have some hair growing back, it's quite short and tufty, I don't mind if you see." Rachel pulled off her wig and chucked it down by her bag. Her natural hair was a light brown, and it was much longer than Thea expected it to be. It was very fine and a bit uneven, but she still looked beautiful.

"Tada!" Rachel giggled.

"Handsome as always."

Rachel smiled and snuggled down under the duvet. Thea placed the treats on the floor and turned off the lamp. She lay down and faced Rachel, she could just make out Rachel's shape in the darkness.

"Goodnight, Tee, sweet dreams." She Reached out and held Thea's hand.

"Goodnight, Rachel" Thea whispered. Rachel did not let go of her hand.

Thea could smell Rachel's perfume, it felt amazing to have her next to her. She held Rachel's hand a little tighter and closed her eyes. She could get used to this feeling.

Chapter 10

Thea woke up to find Rachel sat at the window looking outside, thoughtfully. The sun was shining on her, she looked so angelic.

"Morning sleepy head" Rachel turned to look at Thea.

"How long have you been up? You should have woken me."

"Not long, don't worry. My hips were a bit achy, I had to get up and move about"

"Will the pain stop soon? Now you don't need anymore treatment?"

"I hope so, I am still a little bit sore from the last treatment, that's all."

Thea sat up and stretched.

"I slept really well, it must have been good company."

Rachel smiled sweetly at Thea.

"I had a really fun night, Tee."

"Shall we go and get some breakfast? Smells like mum has some toast on the go already."

"Sounds good, I am just going to go and get dressed."

Rachel put on her wig and headed to the bathroom with her bag. She didn't seem her normal chirpy self. Maybe the falling asleep holding hands thing was too much last night, but Rachel had gone for her hand first. Maybe she expected Thea to let go? Thea hoped she hadn't made Rachel feel uncomfortable. She got out of bed and got dressed in the same leggings and hoodie from the night before. Her hair had stayed quite neatly in the plait, so she didn't bother to re do it. Rachel appeared back in the bedroom, also wearing the same clothes from yesterday. She was smiling, but it looked forced.

"Let's go, Tee, I am starving." She rubbed her belly and carried on downstairs.

"Morning ladies." Thea's dad was in the kitchen making some coffee.

"Mum has just gone to the hardware store, but she has left some toast for you. Jam, peanut butter or just butter, take your pick."

Rachel took a piece of jam on toast, as well as a peanut butter piece, and placed them together like a sandwich.

"Yum." She took a big bite of her jam and peanut butter toasted creation. It did look pretty tasty, but Thea settled for two pieces with jam.

"Do you want to go out today, Rachel?"

"Sorry, Tee. Mum wants me to spend some time with her and dad today. Parents ey?" she sighed.

"That's alright, before I forget, can I get your mobile number? I keep meaning to ask."

"Course you can, pass me your phone."

Rachel put her number in Thea's phone and handed it back to her.

"I might not be on my phone much today, but text me whenever you like. I will reply when I can."

Rachel finished her toasted sandwich and picked up her bag.

"I better head off. Thank you for having me over, Kevin, I've had an amazing time."

"No problem at all young lady, thank you for being such a pleasant guest."

Thea followed Rachel to the front door. Rachel hugged Thea and opened the front door.

"Have a good day, Tee. Say thanks to your mum for me."

"Will do, bye Rachel."

Thea watched Rachel walk down the road, she wasn't bouncing along like normal. Rachel had hugged her goodbye and said she could text her whenever she liked. She couldn't be upset with Thea, surely. Thea checked her contacts for Rachel's name, but couldn't see the name Rachel anywhere. She tried to search for it, nothing. Great, there was something wrong, she didn't even give Thea her number.

Thea shuffled into the kitchen and poured herself some orange juice.

"Rachel is so sweet isn't she? Calling herself your best friend already."

Thea looked at her dad, confused.

"When did she say she was my best friend, dad?"

"Did you not check your phone? I saw that's what she saved her number under on your phone."

Thea grabbed her phone and relooked at the contact list. Right at the top, there it was, the new contact. She had saved it under *Best Friend*. Rachel obviously wasn't annoyed at Thea, but she was upset about something. Thea needed to find out what.

Thea's mum burst through the door struggling with three large tins of paint. Thea ran to her and relieved her of one of the tins.

"Thanks, Tee. Can you take it straight up to the bedroom?".

Thea found her parents room was completely covered in dust sheets. No furniture was visible anymore. She placed the tin by the door and went to go back downstairs.

"Hold your horses, missy. Get some old clothes on, it's painting time."

"Why do I have to paint?" she questioned.

"Because your dad is going into the office today to meet his new boss and I really want to get this done. The walls are already white so at least we don't have to do that first. We can go straight in with the new colour."

Thea looked closer at the tins. Her mum had picked a deep purple, Thea approved of her colour choice.

"Fine, let me go and get changed."

Thea went back to her own room and changed into her old clothes that were already covered in her own paints. She looked over at her easel and saw Rachel had forgotten to take the painting. Thea hoped she did actually like it after all. She decided to send her a message, knowing she might not get a reply for a while.

Hi Rachel. Mum is making me help her paint her bedroom, child slavery! I hope you have a good day. Tee. xx

Thea thought it best not to mention the painting or the sleeping situation for now, not until she knew what was wrong. She made her way back into her parents room, where her mum was already popping off one of the paint lids and pouring the paint into trays.

"Grab a roller Tee, let's get going. You take that wall first, I'll start on this one."

Thea took a roller off the bed and began painting.

"Did you have a nice time with Rachel last night? Sorry I missed her this morning, I set off early to miss any traffic."

"We had a great time, thanks. We made friendship bracelets, look." Thea held her arm in the air so her mum could admire her bracelet.

"Those colours are very you. I'm glad you had a good night. What is Rachel up to today?"

"She is spending some time with her parents today. She didn't seem herself this morning, I'm hoping she's okay."

"I'm sure she's fine. Probably irritated she has to spend the day with her parents and not with you."

Thea hadn't explored that idea. Her mum could be right, she would rather be with Rachel right now, then painting a bedroom with her mum.

After what seemed like hours, Thea started to feel a bit dizzy.

"Mum, this is giving me a headache."

"Oh God" her mum cried, "I forgot to open the windows, no wonder you feel ill. Let's go get some lunch and I will leave all the windows open up here for a while, get some fresh air in."

They made their way to the kitchen to find Grandma maisy was already making lunch for everyone.

"The hard workers return."

"Hi Grandma, you could have come up and said hello."

"I got halfway up the stairs and the fumes nearly killed me."

"Sorry about that mum, I have opened all the windows now."

"No bother, sit yourselves down, I have made some sandwiches. I am heading out after lunch to meet Lily and George for bowls."

"Blimey Grandma, you have a better social life than me" Thea laughed.

"Got to keep going, Theadora. I worry if I sit down for too long, I may never get back up again and I will die in my armchair."

"Mum! Don't talk like that!" Thea's mum cried.

Grandma Maisy winked at Thea and Thea started to giggle.

"There is still some life in me yet, Sue. Don't you worry about that."

Thea ate her lunch and went upstairs to check her phone. No message from Rachel, in fact Rachel hadn't even read Thea's message yet. She must really be busy. She went back down to the kitchen to get a drink.

"Talking of death, have you heard of anyone dying in the village lately, Sue?" "Grandma Maisy asked.

"What a charming topic mum, but no I haven't, why?"

"I saw Layton and Son's funeral car driving up our road earlier this morning."

"No idea, mum. Maybe they were using our road as a shortcut. It can block out some of the busier main roads."

"Very true. Right, I am off. Enjoy painting girls."
Enjoy painting? Enjoy torture more like.

Chapter 11

The rest of the day seemed to go on forever. Thea's painting arm was done in by dinner time and Rachel had still not read her message. She hoped Rachel had actually typed her number in correctly. Thea got through dinner without too many annoying questions from the family, then returned to her bedroom and sat down in front of her easel. She stared at the portrait, hoping Rachel was alright, she had definitely not been herself that morning. Thea changed into her pyjamas and got into bed. She looked at her phone, it was only 8pm, but she was shattered.

She was close to dozing off when she heard her phone ping. It was a message from Rachel.

Hi Tee. I am really sorry for the late reply, my phone died and I didn't realise. I will give you a call in the morning. Night night xx

Thea read the message, then read it again and then again for a third time. She couldn't be mad at Rachel for not knowing her phone had died. Thea smiled at her phone and put it back on the bedside table. She closed her eyes and thought of Rachel, she couldn't wait for her to call tomorrow.

Thea woke suddenly, her phone was ringing loudly. In her sleepy state she assumed it was her alarm, until she opened her eyes properly and saw *Best Friend* on the screen.

"Hello" Thea answered, still not quite sure what was going on.

"Oh, Tee, I woke you up. Call me back when you are up."
"No, no, don't worry, I'm awake." She was barely awake,
her mind hadn't even caught up to what day it was yet.
"Well I am just having some breakfast, and then would you
like to go out today? It is market day in the village, we could
have a wander around."
"Sounds Perfect, Rachel. Give me an hour or so I can have a
shower and some breakfast too."
"Fab! See you in an hour."
Thea hung up and closed her eyes. She was excited, she
really was, it was just hard to show it when she was still half
asleep. She got up, showered, and stood at her wardrobe,
staring at her clothes. This seemed to be a regular occurrence
now. She had never bothered with what she wore before, but
now she was always taking care with how she looked, how
she looked for Rachel. The sun wasn't out and it felt a little
chilly, so no shorts today. She muddled through the hangers
and found a long sleeve, see through white lace top. Her
mum had got it for her at Christmas, and she wasn't very sure
of it. She put on a pale pink strappy top and wore the lace
garment over the top and finished the outfit with some dark
blue skinny jeans and some pink trainers. She marvelled at
herself in the mirror, she was getting better at this.
She set off to the kitchen to get some breakfast, her mum and
Grandma Maisy were sat at the breakfast bar, drinking coffee.
"Tee, that top looks fantastic! I love the coloured top
underneath". Her mum looked so pleased, this was the first
time Thea had actually worn this top out of the bedroom.
"I agree, you look very lovely today, Theadora." Grandma
Maisy complimented.

"Rachel sounded much happier on the phone today, from what I can remember anyway, I was half asleep when she called."

"That's good" her mum replied "She must be looking forward to spending the day with you."

Thea got herself some cereal and joined her mum and Grandma Maisy at the breakfast bar.

"Rachel and I are going to the market today, I haven't been in years."

"It is quite hip down there now, Theadora, not just the farmers selling there anymore. There are jewellery stands, food stands, clothes, it's good for a mooch."

Thea sniggered "*Hip* ey Grandma?"

"Yes, I am down with the kids now."

Thea's mum laughed.

"Oh, mum. Anyway, Tee, you can take £20 out of my purse to take with you."

"Really, mum?" Thea looked shocked and excited all at the same time.

"Course! You did help me paint all day yesterday and you deserve a little treat. Don't spend it all on food though please."

"I won't" Thea sat and ate her cereal, the hour was nearly up, Rachel would be here any minute. She fetched the £20 from her mum's purse, and put it in the front pocket of her rucksack. As she was doing so, there was a knock at the door, Rachel was here. Thea glanced in the mirror in the hallway, checking her hair looked okay. She had left it down for once hoping Rachel would like it. She opened the door to find Rachel was back to the blonde wig, but it wasn't braided today. She had also left it down, flowing down her back, just like Thea.

"That is a fab top, Tee." Rachel reached out to touch the lace sleeve. "Very chic!"

Thea thought Rachel looked incredible today, the best she had ever seen her, other than the slinky nightgown of course. Rachel was wearing a bright orange long gypsy skirt, a black crop top and some crystal studded sandals. The outfit was topped off with a dark denim jacket.

"Have a nice time girls" Thea's mum called from the kitchen.

"Bye, mum."

Rachel and Thea headed towards the market, but Rachel still didn't seem to be as bouncy as normal.

"So, how are things? Did you have a nice day yesterday?" Thea asked Rachel, trying to get any hint of information.

"I am all good, thank you. Yesterday was nice, we all just had a movie day, my mum insisted."

"Well that sounds fun, I helped my mum paint her bedroom all day! My arm is killing today."

"I bet! It is nice that you helped her though, I bet she appreciated it."

"Enough to give me £20 for the market, so I would say it was worth the shoulder ache."

Thea was trying not to stare at Rachel, but she had noticed Rachel was looking quite pale today, she hoped she was feeling alright.

"There is a really nice new jewellery stall at the market, Tee. No way as nice as our friendship bracelets" she winked. "But still pretty lovely things."

"Cool, well we can head there first if you like."

The market was much bigger than Thea remembered, from when she was younger. She could only remember meats, dairy products and fruit and veg being sold here on shabby old wooden tables, but it had definitely had a makeover. Stalls were covered by large colourful gazebos and there was a hotdog stand, a burger bar and a chinese takeaway van, which all smelt fantastic. Thea followed Rachel to the jewellry stand that was under a black gazebo and was covered in glowing fairy lights. All the jewellery sparkled beautifully under the lights.

"I would really love to get a new ring, I had a silver one with a beautiful emerald gemstone in, but it seemed to get lost when we moved house." Rachel snapped.

"Try some on, there are lots of green ones to choose from." Thea tried on a pale pink gemstone ring, she loved it. She looked at the sign for the rings.

All Rings £6 or two for £10.

"Choose the one you would like, Rachel, I will buy it for you."

"Tee, you don't have to do that! Your mum gave you that money to get yourself something."

"I am getting myself something, I am going to get this pink one, it's so pretty. We can have friendship bracelets *and* friendship rings."

Rachel squeezed Thea's hand and gave her the ring she had chosen.

"This one then please!"

Thea paid for the rings and asked Rachel for her hand. She placed the green ring on Rachel's middle finger, her hands were so soft.

"Thank you so much, Tee. It is perfect and I will never take it off." Rachel leant towards Thea and gave her a quick kiss on the cheek. Thea had such a head rush she nearly fell over. Rachel actually just kissed her, well it was a peck on the cheek, but still. Thea turned away from the jewellery stand and spotted a craft stand, full of paints, pencils, sketchbooks, her dream stall.

"Can we head over there next Rachel?"

Rachel turned and saw where Thea was looking.

"Of course! That stand is definitely you!"

Thea wanted to buy everything from the craft stall. They had beautiful embellished sketchbooks and expensive fine line drawing pens. Rachel was also browsing, even though this wasn't really her thing. Thea heard her gasp at something.

"What have you found?"

Rachel didn't say anything, but held up an A4 sketchbook that was a pale pink marble effect and it had the letter T embroidered in rose gold on the cover. Thea also gasped when she saw it.

"Wow!"

"You have to buy it, Tee! It was literally made for you, plus all your sketchbooks are pretty full from what I saw."

Thea took the sketchbook from Rachel, she loved how it also matched her new ring perfectly, but it looked expensive.

"How much for this sketchbook please?" Rachel asked the seller, lifting Thea's arm into the air.

"That one is £10, gorgeous isn't it?" the seller replied. This was too perfect, Thea thought, she had to have it. She handed over her last £10 and put the sketchbook into her rucksack.

"Thank you for finding that, Rachel, it really is perfect."

"Now you can fill it with more paintings and drawings of me." Rachel pouted and did a funny little pose. "Let's go get a milkshake, don't worry, these are on me."

The milkshake stand was very impressive. The flavour list must have had around 50 different flavours on it. Thea chose a white chocolate and strawberry milkshake and Rachel went for a dark chocolate and caramel. It was the best milkshake Thea had ever tasted.

"This is amazing." Thea exclaimed, slurping it all up in under five minutes.

"I am trying to get through every flavour. I have had nine so far, all have been amazing!"

"Might take a while to get through all that lot, and the market is only here once a week."

"That's my year planned out then isn't it." Rachel laughed.

They were sitting on the grass just outside the market entrance, people watching, chatting, laughing. Thea couldn't believe how strong her feelings for Rachel were getting. She just wanted to grab her hand, cuddle her, maybe even kiss her. Not a peck on the cheek, a proper kiss. For now, she was happy enough to just be spending time with her. If today could go on forever, Thea would forever be happy.

Chapter 12

The next few days, for Thea, were perfect. Rachel and Thea had spent these days going for walks, having picnics and playing in the park as it got dark, when all the younger children had gone home. They pushed each other on the swings and cried with laughter when they tried to play on the see-saw that they were obviously too big for.

Each day, Rachel would knock on Thea's door, and they wouldn't return back home until dinner time. Thea was hoping the summer holidays would never end, she was having the best time with her new friend. Thea still hadn't come round to the idea of calling Rachel her *best friend*, Sarah was still her best friend, she just hadn't been able to contact Sarah for over a week now, she couldn't wait to be able to call her.

Thea's parents didn't seem to mind that Thea was out all day, keeping herself entertained, but Rachel's mum called her a lot whilst they were out. It was always the same questions. How far away from home are you? How are you feeling? Rachel would always walk away when she had these phone calls, but Thea could often work out what her mum was asking her, from what Rachel said back. Thea had never thought of her parents as 'cool' parents, but she was now beginning to think they really were.

Thea had noticed Rachel's normal skin colour had not returned to her face, even after three days, but she didn't like to keep asking if she felt alright, as her mum asked her all day already. She had also noticed that Rachel was still taking painkillers everyday, but she tried to wash them back quickly when Thea wasn't looking. Thea would always hear her getting the tablets out of the foil wrapper, even when she was trying to be quiet.

Thea and Rachel would normally head home around 6pm, but on this particular day, Rachel had said she needed to get home and it had only just hit 4pm.

"Sorry, Tee. I feel so tired today, I just didn't sleep very well last night."

Rachel looked like she could have happily fallen asleep, sat up right on the wall outside the village shop, if Thea had let her. Thea thought it best if she walk Rachel home first, before she headed home herself. Thea had offered to walk Rachel home a few times, just to spend more time with her, but Rachel had always refused, telling her to stop being silly.

"Rachel, I am going to walk home with you today, okay?"
Rachel nodded and linked arms with Thea.

"Thank you, Tee, I feel like I need help today, I better not be getting a cold."

Thea was also hoping she wasn't getting a cold, Thea didn't watch to catch it. They walked much slower than normal towards Rachel's house, Rachel held tight to Thea. She would often put her full weight on Thea, which didn't make walking easy, as she was a lot taller than her. Thea had not seen Rachel's house before. It was a stunning thatch cottage, much bigger than Grandma Maisy's house. There was a brand new bright white range rover in the driveway, Thea knew her dad would be jealous of that. They walked up the garden path which was lined with red and white roses, and Rachel knocked on the large olive green front door.

"Are you not allowed to walk into your own house?" Thea laughed.

"I have forgotten my key, like an idiot." Rachel mumbled. Her speech had become very slow. Rachel's mum opened the door. She was a very tall lady, even taller than Rachel and she wore tight jeans, a small top that made it hard to look anywhere but her chest, and some heeled boots. She looked too glamorous to be a mum. She was smiling as she opened the door, but her face soon dropped as she saw the state Rachel was in.

"Rachel? What has happened, Thea? Sorry, I assume you are Thea." She was speaking fast and Thea could detect the panic in her voice.

"She just became very tired and feels like she might be getting a cold. I helped her walk back from the shop."

"Well, thank you Thea, I will take it from here. Probably best to get Rachel to bed. Goodbye." Before Thea could even say goodbye back, her mum had closed the front door. Why was she so worried? Everyone gets a cold. Thea headed back to her own house, she was hoping she would be able to see Rachel tomorrow, she just needed a good night's rest.

When Thea got home, her parents and Grandma Maisy were sitting in the living room watching TV. She sat down on her sofa next to her mum.

"You okay, Tee? You look tired."

"I just basically carried Rachel home, so I am quite tired." Her dad gave her a concerned look.

"You just carried Rachel home?" he asked.

"Well the way I just said that made it sound like I carried her on my back. She started to feel unwell so I let her lean on me as we walked to her house. She thinks she is getting a cold."

"In the summer?" her dad continued to question.

"I don't know dad, stop asking me questions. Maybe it's the flu."

"I am sure she just needs a good sleep." her mum interrupted, seeing Thea was getting irritated. That was normal for Thea when she was tired.

"Thea, why don't you go for a lay down before dinner?"

Thea wasn't one to nap normally, but the idea of going to bed right now sounded amazing. She didn't even bother to change, she took her shoes off and lay on top of the duvet, as her room felt quite warm. She decided to message Rachel before she fell asleep.

Hi Rachel. I hope you are feeling okay. Get some rest and feel better soon xx

Thea didn't think she would get a reply until tomorrow, but Rachel replied straight away.

Thanks for helping me home Tee. I am getting an early night and will message you tomorrow. Night night. xx

Rachel was obviously okay, just feeling a little under the weather. Recently, Thea could only think about Rachel before she went to sleep, but she fell asleep as soon as her head hit the pillow this time.

Thea woke about an hour later, and could smell whatever her mum was cooking downstairs. She couldn't quite work out what it was but it smelt good. She saw she had another message from Rachel. Maybe she was struggling to sleep.

Hi again Tee, just thought I best let you know that my parents and I are going to Cornwall tomorrow for a week. Mum wants us all to go see the family before summer is over. Sorry to tell you at such short notice, we had been having so much fun I forgot we were going. You can still message me as much as you like. See you soon xx

Thea sat up and stared at her phone. She couldn't believe what she was reading. Rachel was going to be gone for a whole week. How could Rachel have forgotten? Thea laid back down and sighed. She had been having the best time with Rachel and now she would be on her own again.

"Tee, are you awake?" her dad called up the stairs.

"Yes, dad."

She made her way downstairs and slumped in the armchair in the living room. Grandma Maisy was sitting doing a crossword puzzle from the paper.

"Why are you looking so miserable, Theadora?" she asked.

"Rachel has just messaged me, she's going to Cornwall for a whole week, tomorrow."

"She must be feeling better for her parents to go ahead with that trip. Takes a good 7 hours from here."

"I guess she must be, but now I'm back to being on my own again. We were having so much fun." Thea looked away, feeling like she might actually burst into tears.

"A week will go by in no time, don't you worry." Grandma Maisy smiled reassuringly.

Thea's mum appeared suddenly in the lounge, she walked ever so quietly.

"Dinner is ready you lot, come on."

Grandma Maisy and Thea continued into the dining room, Thea still felt like she might cry at any minute.

"Did I just hear you say Rachel and her family are going away?" her mum questioned.

"Yes, to Cornwall to see all their family. It is where Rachel used to live."

"Oh, well no bother. Your dad may be back at work, but I won't be until you start back at school, so I am sure we can find some things to keep us occupied."

Great, Thea thought to herself. Spending the summer holidays with her mum, how very uncool. Thea ate her dinner rather quickly, so fast that it didn't go unnoticed.

"Do you have somewhere to be?" Her dad joked.

"No, sorry, I am not being rude intentionally. I have a few ideas for my new sketchbook and I would really like to get started."

"Off you go then, don't let us keep the great artist from her work." her mum teased.

Thea took her new sketchbook from her rucksack and escaped to her bedroom. She already knew what her first drawing would be, Rachel of course. She decided to put Rachel in the outfit she wore when they went to the market a few days ago. Rachel had looked amazing and Thea had the perfect shade of orange paint for Rachel's skirt. She stopped and looked at what she had drawn so far. Thea's feelings had become so strong for Rachel, that her thoughts, drawings and even her dreams had all become about her. Thea realised she couldn't go on, not telling Rachel how she really felt, she needed to know how Rachel felt about *her*. She decided enough was enough and she was going to tell Rachel, when she returned from Cornwall. Thea now had a week to compose herself and work out how she was actually going to tell Rachel, but she would get there somehow, she had to.

Chapter 13

Thea still felt tired the next morning. She hadn't slept very well. In a week's time she could possibly have a girlfriend, an understanding friend, or no friend at all. Who knows what would happen when she told Rachel how she felt. She hadn't really thought how her parents would take it, she was more concerned with the person involved. She checked her phone to find she had received a message from Rachel at 4am that morning.

Hi Tee, I hope this doesn't wake you. Mum is making us set off so early, I am barely awake. I miss you already xx

Missing Thea already must be a good sign, she thought. She replied to Rachel.

Hi Rachel, you really did leave early this morning. I hope the drive isn't too long and boring. Miss you too xx

Thea threw on some old baggy clothes as she didn't need to dress up today and went to find her mum to see what today's plans were.

Her mum was in the kitchen looking through the paper.

"Pottery?" her mum asked.

"Sorry?" Thea replied, looking confused. Her mum hadn't even said hello or good morning yet.

"I am looking at the events page in the village paper. They have a pottery class at the village hall today."

"I paint and draw mum, I have never tried pottery ever, not even at school."

"I know, I thought it would be fun for us to try something new together. Come on, it might be a laugh. If it's pants we can sneak out. It's only a fiver each."

Thea would do anything to meet up with Rachel today, but that was impossible of course, so pottery it was.

"Go on then, I am already in some old clothes. When does it start?"

Her mum looked at her watch.

"In just over an hour. I am going to go and get changed, make sure you have some breakfast."

Her mum disappeared upstairs and Thea made herself some scrambled egg on toast. She could see that Grandma Maisy was sitting in the garden, reading. It was nice to be able to see Grandma Maisy every day and not every five or six months as before. Her mum came back downstairs and picked up her bag.

"Come on Tee, they are only serving tea and coffee at the village hall, so we will go to the shop first and get you a bottled drink to take."

Thea tried to drink coffee every few months. Fancy flavoured coffees were all the rage in London, but no matter what she tried, it was all disgusting to her. Her dad had always told her it's not a bad thing to not like coffee. He told her too many people relied on coffee to stay alive. She put on her shoes and jacket and followed her mum out the house.

"I do love being able to walk everywhere in the village from home." Her mum said.

"It is a lot easier than the tube, trains and buses." Thea replied

"It really is, and the air is so much fresher here." Her mum breathed in deeply. Maybe the move here has been good for the whole family, Thea thought. They nipped in to shop and picked up a bottle of water for her mum and a lemonade for Thea.

The village hall was full of women around her mum's age, no one looked even close to Thea's age. A lady walked up to Thea and her mum.

"Is this your daughter?" The lady asked Thea's mum. "My daughter would never do something like this with me, you are very lucky!"

Thea's mum put her arm around Thea.

"I am very lucky," she said, looking proud.

Thea rolled her eyes, but she was glad she had made her mum happy by coming along to the class. They walked across the hall and both sat down in front of a pottery wheel.

"I am going to be awful at this," her mum laughed "I can just see my clay shooting across the room and hitting the teacher."

"You won't be that bad, mum!"

The teacher stood in the middle of the hall and gave a quick explanation of how to use the pottery wheel, which followed with a demonstration of how to create a simple bowl shape. Thea could see the panic in her mum's eyes. She put her hand on her mum's shoulder.

"No one is watching us mum, everyone is doing their own thing, we got this!"

Thea and her mum began creating their bowls. The clay wobbled all over the place. They got the giggles so bad, they could barely keep the clay on the pottery wheel. No one in the class seemed to be doing very well, the whole group started to laugh at themselves and each other. Thea imagined if this was a class in school, the teacher would be getting super angry at the whole class laughing, but the pottery teacher was also finding it hilarious, having a good laugh with the group.

"When you all take your bowl home, you can tell your families it was an abstract pottery class!" the teacher chuckled.

Whilst all the bowls were in the kiln, food was served to the class. Thea didn't expect the food to be any good, but everyone was given a crusty bread cheese and pickle sandwich and it was delicious.

Thea checked her phone, no reply from Rachel yet. Thea's mum saw she looked disappointed.

"Mum, do you think it's weird that Rachel just forgot she was going on holiday for a week?"

"Well she does seem a bit all over the place sometimes, I don't think she meant to not tell you earlier than yesterday."

"I had spoken to her before about where she used to live, when she told me she really missed the beach. You would have thought she would have said something then, knowing she was going back soon."

"Try not to look too much into it, Tee. Rachel is a lovely girl and she seems very fond of you. She appears bright and early every day to come and get you."

"I guess so. Well I can't wait for her to get back, I am still hoping she might be able to start school again too."

The pottery teacher called across the hall for everyone to come and get their bowls. It was time to paint them. Thea and her mum got the giggles again as they were handed their bowls. Thea's wasn't too bad, a little wobbly around the edges but you could tell it was a bowl. Thea's mum's looked like it once was a bowl that had now been sat on. Her mum held it up and laughed.

"Well I probably won't start up my own pottery business anytime soon!"

"I like it mum. What colour are you going to paint it?"

"I don't think any colour is going to save this thing."

"Why don't you paint it a dark purple to match your room? The way it has flattened slightly makes it look like a jewellery dish."

"You know what Tee, you have a good point there! What a great idea."

Thea chose a teal blue for hers to match her room and some gold to paint a fine pattern on top. She was going to use hers to keep all her hairbands and scrunchies in, as she never seemed to be able to find one. The hall was very quiet whilst everyone was painting, concentrating on their work.

"This has been really fun, mum. I am glad I came along."

"Me too," her mum replied. "I haven't laughed like this in ages. Moving house, finding a new job and living back with my mother after 20 years hasn't been the easiest, I needed today."

Thea hadn't really thought about how the move had affected her parents, she felt she had been quite selfish.

"You can always talk to me mum."

"And you can always talk to me, I hope you know that."

Thea had a weird feeling deep down in her stomach. She really wanted to tell her mum about her feelings for Rachel, how she thought she liked girls and not boys, but she just didn't feel brave enough yet.

"That gold pattern looks so neat and lovely on that teal colour, Tee." her mum praised.

"Thanks. I'm going to keep my hairbands in it."

"Good plan, then you might actually be able to find one for once."

The class finished painting and the teacher told everyone to leave their work to dry. They would all be able to collect their bowls tomorrow.

"Your dad should be home by now, hopefully he or Grandma has started dinner." Her mum stood up and stretched. They had been sitting down all day. Thea checked her phone, Rachel had finally messaged back.

Hi Tee. The drive was very long and it was very boring. We had to stop so many times because it was super hot in the car and mum kept drinking lots of water. I have never known someone need the toilet so much! We are staying at my

*aunty's house but I do have my own room to stay in. Mum
and dad are on the sofa bed in the living room. Hope you had
a good day xx*

Thea thought it was odd that Rachel would have her own
room to stay in and that her parents were sleeping in the
living room. Thea's parents definitely would have made her
sleep on the sofa bed. Thea and her mum were about to walk
home, so she decided to reply to Rachel when she got back.
That was nearly one day down, only six more to go until
Rachel was home and today had actually been really fun.
Like her mum, she was also hoping her dad or Grandma had
started dinner, she was starving.

Chapter 14

When they got home, Thea went straight up to her room to
put her pyjamas on. It was only 5pm but Thea loved
mooching about the house in Pyjamas when she knew she
didn't have to go back out of the house. She sat on her bed
and began to reply to Rachel's last message. She had so
many questions, but she tried to keep things simple, as
Rachel moaned all the time about her mum questioning her
24/7.

*Hi Rachel. I bet you were glad when you finally got there. No
more wee stops! It is great that you have your own room. Are
you seeing much of your family this week or just your aunty?
Me and mum went to a pottery class today. It actually turned
out to be a lot of fun. Can't wait to see you xx*

Thea carried on with her sketch of Rachel in her new
sketchbook. She had only been drawing for five minutes
when her phone went off. It was Rachel.

Pottery? I would have loved to do that! Send me some pictures of what you made, I would have been awful I reckon. Two of my cousins live here too, so I get to see them but they are only 6 and 8 years old. They are quite annoying actually. I will be seeing my grandparents tomorrow, I get to go to the beach, yay! Xx

Thea thought about the last time she had gone to the beach. She hadn't been to a beach in the Uk since she was a toddler. She had been on holiday two years ago in Italy, but the sand at the beach was so hot, she had to wear flip flops all the time. Her mum loved sunbathing for hours, but Thea and her dad would often get bored and walk off to the shops, leaving her mum to sunbathe in peace.

Thea thought Rachel sounded upbeat, she was glad she was getting to see her family. Rachel had told Thea she was used to seeing her grandparents nearly every weekend, she missed them so much.

Thea loved being able to message Rachel whenever she liked now. She also loved how quickly Rachel had replied. Thea decided to reply straight away.

I will send you some pictures tomorrow, we will collect what we made in the morning. I have a cousin who is 5 and he is really annoying, so I know how you feel. Send me some pictures yourself, of the beach. Have a great time xx

Thea could smell Grandma Maisy's special pizzas, she headed downstairs immediately.

"You seem to have a knack for knowing when food is ready, like a bloodhound." Her dad chuckled.

"It just always smells so good. I am glad all three of you can cook, some of the food Sarah's mum tries to prepare is questionable."

"Well sit yourself down, I will bring your food in, Grandma has put a can of cola on the table for you."

"Her teeth will rot drinking all those fizzy drinks" her mum tutted.

"But they taste so good!" Thea opened the can and took a big swig.

"Ahhhhh, lovely."

Her mum rolled her eyes.

"So did you girls have a nice time today?" Grandma Maisy asked as she entered the dining room. Her mum started to laugh.

"It was...different." Thea started to laugh too.

"What are we missing here, Maisy?" her dad asked.

"You will see tomorrow, don't you worry." her mum sniggered.

"So, Rachel messaged me earlier. She is going to the beach tomorrow with her Grandparents."

"Oh I love the beach. We never go enough." her mum sighed.

"Because it always takes blooming ages to get there." her dad replied.

"I have asked her to send me some pictures, so we can have a look when I get some through."

"Lovely, well what shall we do tomorrow then?" Thea's mum asked.

"I have no idea. What are you up to, Grandma Maisy?"

"I am at the bowls club tomorrow, if the weather stays nice."

Thea was chuffed Grandma Maisy was keeping herself busy all the time and seeing her friends. Everyone in the village loved her and looked out for her.

"I do need to go and pick out some new curtains and bedding for our room actually, the current bright yellow ones are clashing nicely with the deep purple walls. We could go into the next town?"

Thea couldn't think of anything better. She would be able to look in proper clothes shops and get lunch out.

"Oh, yes please mum!"

"That's a plan then. We can get you some new school shoes whilst we are at it."

Her dad was smiling at Thea and her mum.

"I love that my best girls get along so nicely." he looked over at Grandma Maisy.

"You too of course, my other special lady."

"I appreciate that Kevin, but you can still do the washing up."

They all laughed. Thea was feeling so grateful for her family. She was now super excited for the shopping trip tomorrow and was nearly another day closer to seeing Rachel. Things were good.

Chapter 15

After dinner, Thea went back to her room to finish her picture of Rachel. She checked her phone, no messages. She knew Rachel would be busy with her family. They were probably having a movie night, playing board games, all the normal family stuff.

Thea fetched her bright orange paint to start Rachel's skirt. Her tongue was poking out as she painted, a normal concentration face for her. Thea didn't mind that Rachel wanted to keep the canvas portrait, but this piece would be for Thea. She had loved Rachel's blonde hair at first, but once she saw the pastel pink bob, she now only ever pictured her with that hair, when she thought about her.

Thea began to yawn, she stopped painting immediately. She had often tried to carry on painting when she was tired and found she always managed to make a mistake, she knew it was best to carry on tomorrow.

She placed her sketchbook on the floor, leaving it open to dry. She got into bed and shimmied right down under the duvet. She hoped Rachel would message her again tomorrow, Thea was really missing her. She lay there, thinking about how she was going to run up to Rachel and give her a big hug as soon as she saw her. She fell asleep, hoping to dream of Rachel. She woke up to her mum tapping her gently.

"Time to get up, Tee. We need to leave in about an hour."

Thea looked at the time on her phone.

"Sorry, mum, looks like I forgot to set my alarm."

"Not a problem, I will go and get some breakfast started whilst you get ready. Bacon rolls okay?" her mum smiled.

Thea heard her stomach rumble.

"My tummy thinks that sounds perfect."

Thea's mum left the room and Thea trudged over to the wardrobe. *Here we go again*, she thought. She didn't have Rachel to impress today, but her mum looked like she had dressed up for a nice day out, so Thea felt she should do the same. It looked warm and sunny outside so she decided to go with her black shorts. She got her white lace top, but wore a bright yellow strappy top under it this time. She wore her pair of sunflower yellow converse to tie the whole outfit together. She tied her hair in the normal messy bun. The smell of the bacon was calling her. She hurried downstairs, her stomach started rumbling again.

"That smells amazing, give me give me!" Thea demanded
"Manors lady!" her mum laughed. "I love all the matching
yellow by the way, you look lovely."

"Thank you, mum. I was thinking earlier, I think gold would
be nice for your curtains and bedding. It will make your room
look super posh."

"Oh I hadn't thought about gold. I have a sample strip of the
purple, so we can see how well it goes with some gold
fabrics. Great idea, Tee." Her mum patted her on the head
like a child, Thea didn't mind. She was enjoying her bacon
roll too much.

They both finished eating and headed off to the car.

"Right, girly time, lets go!". Her mum cheered.

Thea sighed at her mum, but it was great seeing her mum in a
good mood.

The next town wasn't too far away, about half an hour in the
car. Thea could see the large shopping centre towering in the
sky, way before they even got to the carpark for it.

"Mum, do we have to go and get the curtains and bedding
first?"

Her mum could tell Thea wanted to go around all the other
shops first.

"Curtains and bedding are pretty heavy I guess, maybe it
would be best to do that last." She saw Thea smile.

"If you like, you can choose a few bits for your birthday? I
know it isn't until next week, but you get harder to buy for
every year. This way you can choose what you like."

Thea's eyes lit up.

"Really mum? Thank you!"

They parked up and entered the shopping centre. It was a
large glass building and the shops looked endless. It had only

been built the year before, so it was new to both Thea and her mum. They both looked up in awe at the high glass ceilings.

"Wow." Thea marvelled.

"Wow indeed." her mum replied. "Where shall we go first then?"

Thea studied the shopping centre map, pointing here there and everywhere.

"The chocolate shop, oh wait they have a craft shop, two craft shops, oh and that new funky clothes shop!"

"Looks like we have a busy day ahead of us, Tee."

Thea and her mum spent hours wandering the shops, they were all massive. They went into this one clothes shop that was filled with such amazing clothes. Thea, for once, found she wasn't only attracted to baggy clothes. She discovered a very stylish pair of black ripped skinny jeans and a pale blue long sleeved crop top. She tried it on and felt totally transformed.

"Woah, Tee!" her mum made Thea do a spin. "You are really getting a proper womanly figure."

"Mum!" Thea groaned, feeling a little embarrassed. She did think she looked great in the outfit though.

"Why don't you go have a look in the chocolate shop, it's just across from this one. I will go and pay."

"I can wait for you mum, I don't mind."

"It's okay. I know you wanted to look there and I am trying to stick to my diet, I will be hopeless around all that sweet stuff. You go." Her mum handed Thea a five pound note.

Thea skipped away, the smell of chocolate hit her hard as she entered the shop. Everything looked incredible, how would she choose? The shop was sectioned off into three parts, white chocolate, milk chocolate and dark chocolate. White was her favourite, so she headed to the back of the shop. There was so much to choose from. White chocolate buttons, white mice, white chocolate covered biscuits. Her mouth began to water. She spotted a small pink box, tied with a silver ribbon. She turned the box over to read the label.

Four strawberry cream filled white chocolate truffles.

That was it, decision made. She paid for her chocolates and met her mum outside the shop.

"I can smell all that chocolate from out here!"

"I got some white chocolate strawberry truffles. One for me, dad, Grandma Maisy and you, for after dinner. Forget the diet for today!"

"You are thoughtful, Tee. How about we go and get some lunch?"

In the middle of the shopping centre was a beautiful cafe. It was filled with large indoor tropical plants and it had a small stream flowing around the outside which was the home to many multicoloured koi carp.

They found a table and browsed the menu.

"This whole place is so amazing isn't it. I think Rachel would love it here."

"This place does feel very *Rachel.*" her mum replied.

Thea checked her phone, still no message.

"What do you fancy? I will go up and order."

"Um…..Can I please have a cheese and ham toastie and a strawberry milkshake?"

"Coming right up." her mum got up and left the table.

Thea decided to message Rachel. She took a picture of the koi carp that were swimming so gently through the stream.

Hi Rachel. I hope you are having a nice time at the beach. Mum has brought me to this amazing new shopping centre.

Look at the beautiful fishes! Xx Thea attached the picture and sent the message.

Her mum arrived back at the table with a coffee and a bright pink strawberry milkshake. It was topped with whipped cream and a strawberry.

"This place just keeps getting better." Thea laughed.

"Food will be over in five mins, try not to fill up on that thing!"

Thea's mum handed her the shopping bag from the clothes shop.

"Why don't we have a look at what you got?"

Thea looked confused.

"Mum, you saw what I got. I tried it on."

"Just take a look in the bag, Tee."

Thea looked inside the shopping bag. She could see the jeans, the blue top and there was something else. There was a black box tied neatly with a sparkly pink bow.

"What is this mum?" Thea asked, looking excited.

"Open it." her mum insisted.

Thea untied the bow and lifted the lid off the box. It was a delicate rose gold necklace with a small rose gold letter T pendant on it. Thea gasped.

"It is beautiful mum, thank you so much, when did you…?"

Thea thought about her mum ushering her to the chocolate shop.

"Really, thank you."

"I am really glad you like it. Your dad and I thought you deserved something special."

A waitress appeared with their lunch and Thea couldnt believe what was on her plate. Not only was there a cheese and ham toastie, there was salad, some crisps and three tiny pots all filled with different dipping sauces.

"Salad, mum. I feel so posh."

Her mum chuckled.

"I will be more impressed if you actually eat some of that salad."

They finished their lunch and headed towards the home store. Opposite the home store was one of the craft shops.

"Mum, can I go have a look around here whilst you look for what you need? I won't be long."

"Course, course."

Thea couldn't believe how big the craft shop was. There were easily over 300 colours of acrylic paint and a whole wall dedicated to sketching pencils. Thea thought her set of fifteen paint brushes were enough, but according to the shop someone might need a set of fifty. She was browsing the sketchbooks when she noticed something she had never seen anywhere else. It was a small sketchbook. Well, it wasn't small, it was tiny. It must have only been three inches tall. The chocolates had cost Thea £3 and she realised she still had the £2 change in her pocket. There wasn't a price on the sketchbook, it couldn't cost very much, it was hardly a sketchbook at all. She took the miniature book to the till. A boy, who looked no older than Thea, was standing there.

"Excuse me, how much is this please?" Thea put the book on the counter.

The young boy looked at Thea and saw she was holding a £2 coin.

"How much do you have in your hand?" He asked, giving her a smug smile. Thea held up the coin and smiled back.

"For a beautiful lady like yourself, £2.00."

Thea laughed and handed over the money. She didn't know what she found funnier. The fact he had been super cringey, or the fact in her head she wanted to reply *sorry mate, I like girls.*

Thea went and found her mum who was clutching some gold bedding.

"You were so right, Tee. Gold went perfectly! I am just waiting for the shop assistant to bring me the matching curtains. The size I needed wasn't on the hangers."

"Brilliant. Look at this." She held up the mini sketchbook.

"That is extremely cute. That will be a test for you, drawing and painting tiny pictures."

The shop assistant returned and handed her mum the curtains. Thea held her own shopping bag, her mum was struggling to hold her own things. They paid and ambled back to the car. They were all shopped out.

"Thanks for today mum, it has been perfect."

Her mum smiled and put all their shopping in the boot. Thea got in the car and checked her phone, still no reply from Rachel.

Chapter 16

Thea and her mum stopped at the village hall on their way home to pick up their pottery. Thea's mum seemed to get the giggles every time she looked at what she made. When they arrived home, Thea's dad was just pulling up outside the house. Her mum waved at him from the car.

"Perfect timing," she said, "he can help us bring in the shopping."

Thea carefully carried the pottery into the house, leaving her parents to bring in the shopping. She went upstairs and placed her mum's bowl/jewellery dish on the dressing table in her parents room. She placed some of her mum's bracelets and rings into it and it actually looked really pretty. She then took her own bowl into her bedroom and filled it with all the hair bands she could find around her room.

She was chuffed with it. She took a picture and began to compose a message to Rachel, who had still not replied.

Hi Rachel, take a look at what I made, I am really happy with it! Miss you xx

She was hoping Rachel was alright, maybe her phone had died again. Thea's mum called up the stairs.

"Tee!" Where did you disappear to? Grandma Maisy would like to see what you got today."

Thea headed back downstairs, everyone was sitting in the living room. She picked up her bag of goodies from the hallway and went and sat down next to her mum.

"Mum got me some birthday treats today, we had the best time. The new shopping centre is beautiful." Thea explained.

"Well, show me what you got then." Grandma Maisy replied.

Thea took out her jeans and crop top and lay them on the floor.

"Very swish." her dad nodded.

"And, mum got me something very special." She took the lid off the jewellery box and showed her dad and Grandma Maisy the necklace.

"I love it." she continued.

"That is very pretty, Tee. What a lovely gift." Grandma Maisy marvelled.

"Oh and I got this. I think you will like this dad." She held up her tiny sketchbook.

"Oh look at that!" her dad motioned to Thea to bring it over, so she handed it to him.

"You will have to do some delicate artwork in here. I do like that." He handed the sketchbook back to Thea.

"I have a little treat for us all too, but it is for after dinner."

"Talking of dinner, I better get it started." Her mum stood and up walked to the kitchen.

"And I better help." her dad sighed and followed her mum.

"Have you had a nice day, Grandma Maisy?" Thea asked.

"I have thank you. I am glad to be home with a cup of tea now though. I get tired a lot quicker now, but I am doing my best to not stay in the house all day."

"That's great, Grandma. Keep as active as you can, but don't over do it. Rachel hasn't replied to me all day, I hope she's okay." Thea looked at her phone, still nothing.

"You said she would be going to the beach didn't you? Maybe her mum made her keep her phone at the house. Can easily lose things like that when at the beach."

"That's true."

Thea sat and watched a quiz show on the TV with Grandma Maisy whilst she waited for dinner. Grandma Maisy was quite clever, she was shouting out most of the answers correctly. Thea must have only got about two right. Her dad would shout answers every now and then from the kitchen, he was always wrong and Thea and Grandma Maisy would try not to laugh. Her mum came into the lounge.

"Come on ladies, dinner time."

On the menu tonight were some handmade burgers and chips, it looked delicious. Thea devoured her food within minutes, she just wanted to eat the truffles.. She got down from the table and fetched the box from her bag.

"What's this little treat then?" her dad asked.

"Strawberry filled white chocolate truffles!" Thea licked her lips.

"Oh that sounds fantastic." Grandma Maisy's eyes lit up. Thea carefully untied the bow and handed the box around so everyone could take one. Thea bit the top off hers and used her finger to scoop out the strawberry cream in the middle. It was one of the best things she had ever tasted. Everyone was quiet at the table whilst they ate their treat.

"That was scrumptious. Thank you for letting us all have one, Tee." her mum smiled.

"Agreed, that was so yummy!" her dad was also smiling at her.

"I reckon I could polish off a few boxes of those." Grandma Maisy chuckled.

"I think I am going to go and start some mini drawings." Thea got her small sketchbook from the living room and went upstairs. She sat on her bed and started sketching some tiny, delicate flowers. She was just finishing off a primrose when she heard her phone ping.

It was a message from Rachel, *finally.*

I am so sorry, Tee. We went to the beach and I left my phone at home. I felt so sleepy when we got back, I fell asleep for a few hours. The fishes look very pretty and I love the bowl you made. You did an amazing job! I miss you too, so much xx

Thea was so pleased she had finally replied and was glad Rachel was okay. Thea loved messaging her, she messaged back right away.

Hi Rachel, don't be sorry, I hope you had a nice time. We have to go to the new shopping centre when you get back, you will just love it! It has posh shops and cafes, it was brilliant. Also, I miss you more xx

Thea wasn't lying. She didn't think anyone could possibly miss someone as much as she was missing Rachel. She thought about her constantly. She loved that Rachel was missing her too.

Her phone pinged again.

I would love to go with you, it sounds like a great place. I am going to get some sleep now, Tee. I will call you tomorrow xxx

Rachel was going to get some sleep? It was only 7pm and she had just said she had a few hours sleep not long ago. Must have been a very tiring day.

No worries, have a good sleep, sweet dreams xxx

Thea carried on with her drawings, she drew more tiny flowers, a miniature version of Grandma Maisy's house and some little butterflies and bumble bees. Her mum suddenly appeared in her bedroom.

"Tee, I have sorted the new bedding and curtains, want to come and have a look?" She was looking all pleased with herself. Thea got off her bed and made her way to parent's room. Thea gasped as she entered the room.

"Mum, it looks amazing, like a posh hotel suite!"

"Only because I went for the gold like you suggested. Thank you for setting up the jewellery dish too, it doesn't look half bad now."

"The whole room looks fab mum, I am glad you love it, too."

Her mum put her arm around Thea's shoulders and gave her a squeeze.

"I think I'm going to go to bed now. I didn't realise it had got so late, I lose track of time completely when I'm drawing"

"Goodnight Tee." Her mum kissed the top of Thea's head. Thea changed into her pyjamas and got into bed. She couldn't wait for Rachel's phone call, she hoped Rachel wouldn't make her wait all day.

Chapter 17

Thea woke up the next day, feeling energised and ready for the day. She must have had a good night's sleep. She checked her phone, no messages, but she knew Rachel would be calling at some point.

She mooched downstairs still in her pyjamas. Her dad had already gone to work and her mum and Grandma Maisy were in the kitchen. Grandma Maisy was putting on her shoes and jacket.

"Off out Grandma?" Thea asked.

"Morning Theadora. I am going to the village hall today, book club."

Thea had no idea Grandma Maisy even went to a book club.

"Well have a nice time. What are you up to today mum?"

"Seeing as we had such a busy day yesterday, how does a movie or box set day sound?"

Thea loved the idea of a TV day, she loved films and fiction series and hopefully this meant her mum had bought some snacks. Grandma Maisy headed for the front door.

"Have a nice day girls, I will see you later." Thea hugged Grandma Maisy goodbye.

"I will have to order you some school shoes online. I said we would get you some when we went shopping, but we were obviously having too much fun, we both forgot."

"Oh yeah!" Thea remembered her mum had mentioned it the night before they went to the shopping centre.

"What shall we watch today then, mum?"

"That new Crime series *Unwanted* is available on catch up now, how about that?"

Thea and her mum loved crimes series and documentaries, this sounded like a good choice to Thea.

"Great. Are there any snacks?" Thea asked hopefully.

Thea's mum rolled her eyes and went back to the kitchen. She reappeared with popcorn, crisps and sweets in her arms. Thea smiled, her mum knew how to plan a good TV day. They watched two episodes, each an hour long. They had been glued to the TV since it started. Thea's mum popped to the toilet before they started the third episode. Thea checked her phone, nothing yet. Thea's mum re-entered the lounge with a plate of crackers topped with cheese and some bottles of sparkling water.

"We do need to eat some proper food too." her mum explained.

Thea helped herself to a few crackers and pressed play on the next episode.

Two hours later, two more episodes down, Grandma Maisy arrived home. She looked into the lounge and tutted at all the food on the coffee table.

"Theadora, are you still in your pyjamas?" she questioned.

Thea looked down at herself.

"Oh, I guess I am."

Grandma Maisy tutted again and walked away to the kitchen. Thea and her mum giggled.

"I think four episodes is enough for now, Tee. Maybe we can watch another after dinner?"

"Yeah, no problem. I will go get dressed, although it seems pointless now!"

Thea went up to her room and checked her phone again. Still nothing. The day was getting on and she had assumed Rachel would have called her by now. Maybe she should message her, it might remind Rachel she was meant to call Thea, but did that look desperate? She was unsure of what to do, she decided to leave it and give Rachel a bit more time. Thea got dressed into clothes that pretty much resembled her pyjamas anyway. She went and sat at her easel, the last of today's sunlight was shining in on the portrait of Rachel. Thea couldn't believe how much stronger her feelings were getting, even though Rachel wasn't even there. Being able to miss Rachel had obviously shown how much she really did like her. She stroked the painting, her emotions were all over the place. She had wanted to tell Rachel how she felt, but now it seemed like more of a need. For her own sanity, she couldn't keep this bottled up any longer.

Thea's phone started to ring, Rachel! She didn't even check who was calling, she quickly answered the phone.

"Hello!" she cried.

"You sound excited," her mum said.

"Mum?" Now Thea was really confused. "Why are you ringing me from downstairs?"

"I am right at the top of the garden and your dad called to say he is stopping at the indian takeaway on the way home. I couldn't be bothered to walk all the way up to you to ask what you wanted, it was easier to call."

Thea laughed.

"Makes sense I guess. Can I please just have a chicken korma and some pilau rice, thanks."

"Perfect, he won't be long. Bye!"

Thea hung up, her mum had lost the plot, she thought. Thea couldn't take it anymore, she had to message Rachel.

Hiya Rachel, I hope you are having a nice day. Mum and I have had a binge food TV day, it has been really good. Speak soon xx

She started drawing in her mini sketchbook. She began a rough outline of herself holding hands with Rachel. It was really hard to draw people so small, she decided to not bother with faces. She created a border of tiny flowers around the figures in the picture. She held the sketchbook close to her chest and breathed deeply.

Please hurry home Rachel she thought to herself. She heard her dad come though the front door, the smell of the indian takeaway wafted to her bedroom, she didn't need to be called, she was already on her way to the dining room.

"You are keen" her dad laughed, placing Thea's meal in front of her."

"Can't keep me and food apart dad" she replied, tucking into her korma.

"Have you heard from Rachel yet?" Grandma Maisy asked.

"No, not yet. I'm sure she will message later" she was feeling hopeful.

"You girls can watch another episode of your program if you like" Grandma Maisy offered. "I am going to go up to my room and get started on the new book I have been given to read for the book club."

"I need to go and have a shower after dinner so you have the living room to yourselves." her dad chimed in.

"Cool!" Thea and her mum both cheered.

Everyone finished up eating and her dad offered to wash up before his shower, leaving Thea and her mum to take over the TV. They said goodnight to Grandma Maisy and got comfortable on the sofa, Thea's mum covered them with a soft fleece blanket.

They ended up watching two more episodes, not just one, the program was too good to turn off. Thea's mum looked at her watch.

"Blimey it's getting late. I better go make your dad's lunch for work tomorrow. Shall we carry on tomorrow?"

"That is fine with me mum, but we have to watch another tomorrow, I am dead certain I know who the killer is now."

"You always guess the killer, I still have no idea." Her mum went off to the kitchen. Thea shouted goodnight from the lounge to her mum and went back up to her bedroom. Still nothing from Rachel and it was now 10pm. She knew Rachel would probably be asleep by now if yesterday was anything to go by. How could Rachel have forgotten her? Even after she messaged her earlier. She slumped down on her bed and felt like she wanted to cry. She tried to tell herself to stop being so silly. Rachel was on holiday with her family, Thea shouldn't expect Rachel to be at her beck and call. She tried her hardest not to, but she cried anyway. She needed to speak to Rachel, to see her, to tell her.

Chapter 18

Thea had an awful night's sleep. She kept waking up and thinking about Rachel. She checked her phone at 2am, 4am and finally 7.30am, but there were no messages. She rolled over and looked out her window from the bed, it was dark and drizzly outside. It reflected how she was feeling pretty well. She decided she fancied just staying in bed today. She got right under the duvet and dozed off for another couple of hours. The rain had become so heavy, it caused Thea to wake up.

"Tee." her mum knocked on her door and stepped inside her bedroom. "Are you getting up today?" she asked.

"I don't really feel like it." she mumbled from under the duvet.

"Ok well I have bought you some toast." Her mum placed the plate of toast on Thea's bedside table and left the room. Thea appeared from under the duvet and looked at the toast, jam, her favourite. She attempted a few bites and then gave up, she really wasn't hungry.

She thought about messaging Rachel again, but thought that made her look pathetic and desperate. She read the last messages she had sent, nothing odd, nothing rude. Why wasn't she replying?

She hid back under the duvet and closed her eyes. She felt like crying again. Thea hadn't even known this girl for three weeks, why was she so obsessed with her? Maybe all these new feelings for a girl were throwing her emotions all over the place. She dozed off again and this time woke to Grandma Maisy knocking on the door.

"Theadora, it's lunchtime, are you coming down?"

Thea groaned but she was feeling quite hungry now and her toast was definitely not edible anymore.

"I will be down in a minute." she replied.

She got out of bed and threw on some tracksuit bottoms and a hoodie, she didn't even bother with her hair. She went down to the kitchen to find her mum had made her an egg and bacon sandwich.

"Are you feeling okay, Tee?" her mum asked, looking concerned.

"I just didn't sleep very well." she sat and began to eat her lunch.

"How's Rachel doing?" her mum sat next to her.

"Don't know, don't care, she doesn't care."

"What's brought all this on?" her mum was glaring at her now.

"Well she can't be bothered to reply to me so why should I care if she's doing okay?"

"Don't be like that, Tee. She's just busy with her family, she will get round to it in the end."

"Maybe" Thea groaned. "I'm going back upstairs."

"To do what?" her mum questioned.

"I am going to do some painting." She put her plate in the sink and went back to her room. She got straight back into bed and hid under the duvet, the rain was still very loud. She must have fallen back asleep and for a while too, it was nearly dark outside when she woke. She sat up and checked her phone, nothing. She felt so let down, what had she done wrong? Thea realised she hadn't had a drink all day, she was craving some juice. She headed down to the kitchen and saw her mum, dad and Grandma Maisy were all sitting in the lounge, in silence, her mum's face was looking red.

"Thea, can you come in here for a minute."

Thea? Her mum hadn't called her Thea in years, not unless she was in trouble.

"I am just getting a drink, hang on." She carried on to the kitchen feeling anxious. She got her juice and slowly walked back to the lounge, not sure she wanted to know what was going on. She sat down next to her mum, her dad and Grandma Maisy were on the opposite sofa.

"Everything okay, mum?" Thea asked, she was starting to feel a bit scared. Everyone was looking so serious.

"Well, Tee, it's Rachel, her mum called me about an hour ago."

"I hope you told her to tell Rachel to message me back!" Thea laughed, but nervously.

"Tee." her mum grabbed her hand. "Tee, Rachel has passed away. She passed away last night."

Thea stared at her mum. She didn't blink, she didn't breathe, her head felt like it was filling with smoke, she couldn't see straight.

"But she, she was going to, but she's on holiday? I don't understand."

"Calm down, Tee, it's okay to feel confused." her dad was trying to smile at her, but looked like he was holding back tears.

"But it doesn't make sense. She said her last appointment had gone well, she said she didn't need a check up for 6 months, why did she lie to me?" Thea was getting worked up, she didn't understand what was happening.

"Her mum explained it all to me, Tee. At her last appointment the family were told the treatment wasn't working and that the cancer had spread to her spine and various other places around the body. There was nothing else they could do, sweetheart."

"The poor girl." Grandma Maisy was shaking her head. "The day I saw Layton and Son's funeral car, they must have been at hers. Imagine having to plan your own funeral at 15."

Thea thought about what Grandma Maisy had just said, it must have been the day Rachel said she was having a movie day with her parents. Thea put her head into her hands.

"I don't get this mum, why has this happened? I don't know what to do."

Thea's mum pulled Thea close to her and hugged her tightly, she stroked her head softly.

"No one knows why these things happen, Tee. It's horrible and very sad and I am so sorry."

"Wait, so this holiday wasn't planned at all? She went to Cornwall, to die?" Thea felt like she was going to throw up, she held her stomach.

"Yes, Tee. Her mum said Rachel deteriorated much quicker than they thought, the day you walked her home, they knew they had to get down there as soon as possible."

"I can't believe this is happening, I was meant to...I didn't even get to tell her." Thea stood up suddenly. She wanted to vomit, scream and run away all at the same time.

"Didn't tell her what, Tee?" her dad was looking right at her, she had never seen him look so sad.

"I can't do this, it's not happening, this is *not* happening." Thea ran to her room, she threw herself onto the bed and screamed into her pillow. She felt awful. There she was all day, hating Rachel for not replying, when yesterday she was actually dying, and she wasn't even alive to message her back today. Thea's head began to pound, her whole body ached. She took off her friendship ring and held it tight in her hand.

"Im sorry, Rachel, I'm so sorry, please forgive me." Tears were streaming down her face, she was struggling to breathe. "I think I *love* you" she cried. Rachel would never know how she felt, Rachel had broken Thea's heart, and she wouldn't ever know. Thea could hear her parents at the bottom of the stairs.

"Kevin, just leave her for a while, she needs some time."

"I am just worried about her, Sue. I have never seen Thea like that, not even when your dad died."

Thea hid further under the duvet, she didn't want to see anyone.

"I'll go up when dinner's ready" she heard her mum say "but understand she will probably just want to stay in her room." Thea never wanted to leave her bed again let alone her room. She had so many questions, questions she would now never have an answer to. Why didn't Rachel tell her the truth about being so unwell? She did think Thea was too immature to understand? Thea began crying again, she didn't even get to say goodbye. She rolled over and looked at her sketchbook. It was still open, where she left it, Rachel's bright orange skirt was the only thing Thea could make out through teary eyes. Thea couldn't believe she was never going to see her again, it didn't seem real. She stroked her friendship bracelet and whispered to herself.

"Please don't leave me." she cried. She stayed hidden far under the duvet, she was broken.

Chapter 19

Thea woke up feeling hot and sweaty, still right under the duvet. It was 11pm. Her parents had obviously decided to leave her to sleep. She looked out the window from her bed and saw the sky had cleared, the moon was shining brightly into her room. She kept staring out the window, she felt so empty. She wanted to cry, but she didn't even have the energy to do that.

"Why did you leave me?" she whispered, still staring.

She got up to go to the bathroom. On her way back to her bedroom, her mum appeared at her parents bedroom door.

"Tee?"

Thea jumped slightly, her mum had startled her.

"Hi, Mum" Thea sniffed.

"Let me take you back to bed, I can't sleep."

Thea wasn't in the mood to disagree, she stumbled back to her bed, her mum following closely behind. Thea got back into bed, her mum sat next to her and held Thea's hand. She could see her mum had been crying.

"Sorry for the state of me, Tee. I have been more upset at the thought of you being so upset."

Thea squeezed her mum's hand.

"It's okay".

"I wish I knew what to say, it's such a shock."

"Well, it shouldn't have been a shock, she should have told me what was happening mum." Thea could feel herself tearing up again.

"Tee, she probably just wanted her last days to be filled with fun and laughter and by the sounds of it, you made that happen."

Thea felt selfish again, of course Rachel didn't want her last weeks to be full of sadness, she just wanted to have fun.

"Mum, I needed to tell her something really important, and now I can't, I just don't know what to do."

"What did you need to tell her? Can you tell me?" her mum asked.

Thea closed her eyes and took a deep breath, she was going to tell her mum the truth.

"I liked her mum" she blurted out rather quickly. Her mum looked confused.

"Well of course you liked her, she was your friend, I liked her." she smiled.

Thea took another deep breath.

"No, mum, I *really* liked her. Like how a girl should like a boy, that's how I liked Rachel." She could see her mum's face developing from the confused look to a smile.

"*Oh!* I see what you mean."

"Is that okay, mum?" Thea tried to work out what her mum was thinking.

"Is that okay? What kind of question is that? I couldn't care less if you liked boys, or liked girls, as long as you are healthy and happy, I am happy."

Thea burst into tears.

"I will never get to tell her mum, she will never know how I felt about her, why does it hurt so much?"

Thea's mum laid down beside Thea and put her arm around her.

"Love hurts, don't let anyone ever tell you anything different. What you are feeling is normal and it's terrible. Worse than terrible." She kissed Thea's head. Thea snuggled right into her mum.

"I can't do this mum, I can't not ever see her again." Thea began to get worked up again.

"Calm down, calm down." her mum held Thea tighter. "You will get through this, You can cry as much as you like, scream as much you like, just know we are all here for you, no matter what."

Thea was so thankful her mum had come in. The pain of Rachel's death was destroying her inside, but she had finally told her mum her biggest secret, and that made her feel so much better. She felt silly for not confiding in her before.

"Do you want me to leave you alone?" her mum asked softly.

"No, please stay." She continued to snuggle into her mum, she just needed someone to be there.

When Thea woke the next morning, her mum was still there, but awake. She was looking at Thea.

"Your bed is so much comfier than mine. Do you think your dad would mind if I just stayed in here every night?"

"He wouldn't mind but I would." Thea smiled.

"How are you feeling?" her mum sat up.

"Crappy, but thank you for last night mum, thank you for making me feel so normal."

"You will never be normal." her mum winked "But I know what you mean. You can like or love whoever you want to, it makes no difference to me, or your dad for that matter."

Thea hadn't thought about her dad. Telling her mum was one thing but she didn't know if she was brave enough to speak to him about it. Thea's mum noticed the concern on Thea's face.

"Would you like me to talk to him for you?"

Thea looked at her mum, she could have sworn she could actually read her mind sometimes.

"Yes please, that would be great."

Her mum gave her a hug and got out of Thea's bed. "I'll see you downstairs."

Thea sat up and looked around her room. So many things already reminded her of Rachel. She saw her lace top in the washing basket, probably won't be able to wear that again, she thought. The sweetie wrappers in her bin reminded her of the sleepover, seeing Rachel in that silky nightie. Thea felt flushed, and then upset. She could hear her mum talking to her dad in the kitchen, but wasn't sure if it was *the talk*. She got up and put on some clean jeans and a baggy t-shirt. She didn't bother with her hair again, it probably looked like a birds nest at this point, but she didn't care.

She slowly crept downstairs, trying to work out what her parents conversation was about, but it seemed they had now stopped talking. She carried on into the kitchen and her dad came bounding up to her. He held her close and squeezed super tight.

"Tee, you have to know that your mum and I will always be here to support you."

Yep, her mum had told him. Thea squeezed him back.

"I am sorry that you have to go through this, but we are all here okay?"

She looked up to see her dad was actually crying. She had not even seen him cry at Grandpa's funeral. She felt herself tearing up again.

"I love you, dad."

"And I love you more. Don't ever change, promise me?"

"I promise."

Chapter 20

Thea spent the rest of the day cosying up on the sofa watching TV. She switched from programme to programme, not really concentrating on anything. Her mum had bought her in some lunch, but Thea had only taken a couple of bites. She went through moments of crying and felt guilty if something on the TV made her laugh. She could hear her mum on the phone in the kitchen, it didn't sound like a normal catch up phone call.

"Yes, Claire, no problem, how sweet, I will sort it with Thea." she heard her say.

Thea tried to think, she didn't know Claire, maybe it was something to do with school. Her mum came into the living room.

"Thea, I have just been on the phone to Claire, Rachel's mum."

Thea realised she hadn't even known Rachel's mum's name, she wondered what she had asked her mum to sort.

"She was saying something about a portrait you painted of Rachel?" her mum continued.

"Yes, it's in my room, Rachel had wanted to keep it."

"Well sometimes at funerals, photographs of the person are put in front of the coffin. Rachel said she would like the portrait instead, but I told Claire it is up to you."

Thea didn't really know what to think. She felt honoured that Rachel wanted the portrait at her funeral, but it felt odd knowing everyone attending would see it.

"Yes, they can use it mum. It is important we do exactly what Rachel wanted." Thea felt this was the best option, she wanted the funeral to be perfect for Rachel.

"Brilliant, her mum will be chuffed. I will pop to George's shop this afternoon, I think he sells bubble wrap."

"Why do you need bubble wrap? Can't we just bring it when we go to the funeral?"

Thea's mum sat down next to Thea and sighed.

"Tee, we can't attend the funeral, I am so sorry. It is just too far away, the funeral is going to be in Cornwall so all her family can attend."

Thea suddenly felt sick. First she hadn't even known her friend, her crush, was dieing and now she wouldn't even get to say goodbye. She felt tears trickling down her cheeks.

"I know, Tee. I am so sorry, but maybe on the day of the funeral we can have our own little memorial ceremony, how does that sound? We could plant something special in the garden to remember her by."

Thea liked the idea, but it wasn't making her feel better.

"This is all so crap, mum." She wiped her eyes with her sleeve.

"I know, it is totally crap. The funeral is only in a couple days, they didn't want to wait too long, so I better get this portrait posted out today for delivery tomorrow. Do you want anything from the shop?"

"No thank you." Thea mumbled. She got further under the blanket on the sofa and looked back at the TV.

Her mum left to go to the shop and Thea realised she was in the house on her own. Watching TV was not taking her mind off anything, so she went up to her room. She sat at her easel and gazed upon the portrait of Rachel. She couldn't believe Rachel wanted it at her funeral. Thea smiled, Rachel really must have loved it. She stroked the painting and she began to cry again. Her mum appeared at her bedroom door, Thea jumped.

"Sorry, Tee, you can blame Grandma for getting the creaky stairs fixed."

Her mum placed some bubble wrap, brown paper, tape and scissors on Thea's bed.

"It is a stunning painting, shall we get it sent off?" she asked, holding Thea's shoulder.

Thea took a deep breath and blew a kiss at the portrait. She handed it to her mum, who wrapped it gently and so neatly.

"I better get back out to the post office sharpish. Get yourself back downstairs, I left you something."

Her mum hurried down the stairs and out the door, the post office would be closing soon. Thea stared at the empty easel, it didn't look right without the portrait. She headed back downstairs and noticed a large bar of white chocolate and a bottle of cola on the coffee table. She smiled and sat back down on the sofa. She had no idea how she would get through this if she didn't have her mum. She had just opened her chocolate bar when her dad walked through the door.

"Hi Tee, how are you doing?" he asked, sitting next to her.

"Not great but the chocolate is helping." She broke off a couple of squares and gave them to her dad.

"Thank you very much, I could get used to coming home to chocolate every day." he chuckled. "Where was mum speeding off to? I saw her driving out as I came down our road."

"Rachel told her mum she would like the portrait I painted of her to go in front of the coffin instead of a photograph. Mum needs to get it there by tomorrow."

"Wow, what an honour, Tee. I didn't get to see it!."

"I have a picture on my phone, I will show you later."

Thea's dad put his arm around her.

"Good. Well I am very pleased. I am sorry we can't go to the funeral. Your mum did let me know that she told you that, but we will have a special day here, I have booked the day off work."

Thea turned and gave her dad a big cuddle. She really loved that her parents were being so supportive. Grandma Maisy appeared five minutes later, she looked very tired. She slumped into the armchair in the living room and kicked off her shoes.

"Are you alright Grandma Maisy?" Thea asked, looking slightly concerned.

"Don't worry about me, I thought it would be good for me to power walk back from the bowls club, you know, get the heart racing a bit. Won't be doing that again." she sighed.

"Please be careful." Thea smirked.

"More to the point, how are you doing, Theadora?"

"I am okay, mum and dad have said we can do something special on the day of Rachel's funeral as we can't go."

"Ah yes, your mother and I are heading to the garden centre tomorrow. You can come and choose a plant for Rachel, anything you like."

Thea wasn't sure what plant she wanted, she just knew it had to be bright, really bright. Her mum arrived home, looking a little flustered herself.

"Those road works, honestly. They seem to be everywhere at the moment! Got to the post office four minutes before it closed. All sorted now though."

"Mum catch!" Thea shouted, chucking a square of chocolate to her.

"Brill, needed that." her mum ate the chocolate and went off to the kitchen. Grandma Maisy turned to look at Thea and winked. Thea handed her some chocolate too.

"Ta very much, can't leave the oldies out!"

Thea laughed. She was still hurting inside, but her family were helping her through this, she couldn't ask for anything more.

Chapter 21

When Thea went to bed that night, she didn't feel the need to cry. She wasn't over Rachel's death, she had cried on and off all day, but all the upset had tired her out so much, she pretty much fell asleep as soon as her head hit the pillow. She woke the next day feeling quite excited. She was going to find the prettiest, brightest flower to plant for Rachel. She got dressed and brushed her hair for the first time in three days, it took a while. Her mum called up the stairs.

"Tee, we are leaving in about fifteen minutes."

Thea picked up her tube of orange paint and went down to the kitchen. Her mum and Grandma Maisy were just finishing off their coffee.

"Would you like to eat something quickly before we go?" her mum asked.

"No I am okay, I just want to get going, can you put this in your bag please mum?" She handed her mum the paint.

"I won't ask, but yes."

They all got in the car and headed for the garden centre. It was quite a big garden centre, filled with beautiful plants and garden ornaments.

"Mum can I have my paint now please?"

Her mum handed her the tube and realised what Thea was doing.

"Over there." her mum pointed to a section of bright orange flowers. Thea smiled and made her way over to them. They were all so beautiful, but she needed to find the perfect one. She found orange lilies, marigolds and poppies, but none were quite the right orange. Her mum tapped Thea on the shoulder and pointed towards a bright orange daisy gerbera plant. Thea held her paint tube up to the flower and gasped, it was perfect.

"Oh mum, that one, for sure, it is stunning."

"Then the daisy gerbera it is." her mum picked up the plant pot and they went off to find Grandma Maisy, who was looking at some garden ornaments.

"Over here! I have found something!" she waved her arm in the air so Thea and her mum could see her behind the rows of plants.

When they got to Grandma Maisy, she was holding a small blue and yellow butterfly ornament that had a letter R on the pebble the butterfly was perched on. Thea looked at the shelf where Grandma Maisy had picked it from. There was a butterfly ornament for every letter of the alphabet.

"How about one of these to go by the flower, Theadora? It is very pretty."

"It looks great Grandma Maisy, thank you for finding it. Is that okay, mum? To get the plant and the butterfly?"

Thea's mum smiled and gave Thea a kiss on the head.

"Of course, they will look lovely together."

Grandma Maisy picked up a few packets of seeds and they went to go and pay for everything. Thea was happy she had found the exact flower she was looking for, she was going to look after it as best she could. When they arrived back home, Grandma Maisy put the plant in a tray of water and left it out in the garden.

"It will be fine there until we plant it tomorrow." she said, giving Thea a reassuring smile.

"What time is the funeral tomorrow, mum?" Thea asked.

"It is at twelve o clock, so we will plant the flower around then, okay?"

Thea started to feel quite down again, the flower was beautiful, but it could never bring Rachel back. She went up to her room, sat on her bed and cried. She wondered when the pain would go away, if it would ever go away. Her dad had told her he missed his parents every single day. Thea knew she would miss Rachel every day. She lay on her bed and began to think about the first time she saw Rachel. She was trying to think if she had ever found a girl attractive before. She had always thought other girls were pretty, girls in school and women she saw on the TV, but she had never fancied them. Rachel had definitely been the first to make her feel this way. She looked over at the empty easel, she wondered if she would get the painting back, or maybe Rachel's parents would want to keep it. She felt rude having to ask for it back, she would have to wait and see. Her mum knocked on her door and came into the room.

"I have made you a sandwich, you didn't have any breakfast, you must be starving."

"I wish I was." Thea sighed. Her mum could see she had been crying again.

"I know, it hurts and it will for a while. Not exactly what you want to hear but I don't want to lie to you. I still cry sometimes about my dad, I miss him so much, but you just need to think about the great times you had with Rachel and be thankful for that."

"I am thankful, I had already got my hopes up about her starting school with me, I wouldn't be as nervous. I wasn't nervous to begin with about starting a new school, but now I can't think of anything worse, especially now I have come out about how I feel about girls."

"You know you don't have to tell anyone about your private life, you can tell people when you are ready or when you feel close enough to them, that will always be your choice."

Thea wasn't sure she wanted anyone knowing. Sarah would be back home tomorrow, what was she going to say to her? She would worry about that when it came to it.

"Tee, I know what you are going to say already, but I did see a poster up in the shop about a new youth club starting at the village hall. It's for ages fourteen to sixteen, it might be good to meet some people that are at your school."

Thea couldn't think of anything worse. Being in a hall with a load of people she didn't know and most of them were probably already friends. She looked at her mum and rolled her eyes.

"Alright, alright, I was just mentioning it."

Her mum got up and left the room, Thea thought about the youth club, she groaned and laid back down on her bed. That was something else she could have done with Rachel. She looked at the sandwich her mum had bought up, it did look delicious and she had started to feel peckish. She ate the whole thing in less than five minutes, she really was hungry. She laid back down on her bed and felt like she could go for a nap. She had been sleeping so much lately, but she didn't feel like doing anything else. She didn't even fancy drawing or painting, or reading which she hadn't done in weeks. She awoke a couple of hours later, it was still light outside. She could hear all the family sitting in the garden, chatting away. She prised herself from her bed and went out to the garden.

"You look sleepy." her dad stated.

"I just woke up." she yawned. She sat on one of the garden chairs, even though it was getting later, the sun still felt warm on her face.

"So mum was telling me about this new youth club."

Thea rolled her eyes again.

"Dad, I have already made my feelings clear to mum about that."

"I know, but just think about it, alright?"

"When does it start anyway?" Thea asked, pretending to care.

"On Friday, 7pm." her mum interrupted.

Thea closed her eyes, the sun felt so nice.

"I think I have found the perfect place for Rachel's flower, Theadora." Grandma Maisy said proudly. Thea opened her eyes to see where she was gesturing. Grandma Maisy was pointing over to where she had planted a rose bush for her Grandpa.

"They can keep each other company, what do you think?"

"Sounds great, Grandma Maisy, thank you."

Chapter 22

That night, Thea did not sleep at all. She had nightmare after nightmare about Rachel's coffin going into the ground. She would wake up sweating and gasping for air. She was actually quite glad she wasn't going to the funeral. Her last nightmare had forced her to wake up at 6.30am, she decided to not go back to sleep. She picked up her sketchbook and began to draw. She drew the outline of the orange daisy gerbera. She then drew a tiny Rachel sitting in the middle of the flower. She gave her delicate wings and a dress made of leaves and petals. She also drew a butterfly resting on the flower. She put her sketchbook on her easel and hunted through her paints. She picked a blue and yellow for the butterfly to match the ornament, some different shades of pinks and greens for Rachel's dress and the bright orange for the flower.

Thea checked the time, it was 9am. She had been painting for hours. Her mum came into her bedroom and stood behind her. "That is stunning, Tee. You are just brilliant and what a lovely idea making Rachel into a fairy. Maybe that's what she is now." She squeezed Thea's shoulder. Thea liked that idea, that Rachel had passed on and become a fairy, even if it did sound a bit childish.

"Did you want to say anything at the memorial we are holding today? Grandma Maisy has asked George and Lily along if you don't mind, they really enjoyed chatting with Rachel."

"That's okay mum, but I don't really want to say anything, you can though."

"Alright, I will have a think."

Her mum left the room, leaving Thea to paint. She carried on painting until it got closer to twelve. She knew it would turn twelve o'clock at some point today, but she kind of hoping time would stop so it never arrived. She wasn't sure if she was meant to wear black or if she should wear what she wanted. She decided on some black skinny jeans, a black cardigan with a bright coloured t-shirt underneath. Rachel would have hated all black. She looked out of her bedroom window and could see her mum, dad, Grandma Maisy, George and Lily all walking up the garden path. It felt odd, like their own mini funeral was happening in the garden. She was feeling sick and like she wanted to cry already, but she held it together and went down to the garden. Everyone was smiling at her as she came up the path. She realised this was the first time she had seen Lily since they moved here. Lily gave her a big hug.

"It is lovely to see you Theadora. Not for the best reason, but still nice."

"Nice to see you too, Lily, thank you for coming and you George."

George gave Thea a little salute. Grandma Maisy was holding the butterfly and the flower. Thea could feel herself beginning to crumble and her face must have shown it as her dad held her hand. Her mum began to speak to everyone.

"Afternoon everyone, thank you for coming to our little memorial for Rachel today. It is a shame we can't be at Rachel's funeral, but it is nice we can do this together. Rachel was only in our lives a few weeks, but she became very close to our Thea and made her very happy. Her personality and energy would light up any room she entered."

"Including my shop." George smiled.

Thea could feel tears falling down her face, her dad kept hold of her hand and gave her a tissue.

"We are going to plant this daisy gerbera in memory of Rachel today right next to my dad's roses." Thea's mum patted one of the roses on Grandpa's rose bush.

"Thea, Grandma has already dug the little whole in the soil, would you like to put the plant in?"

Thea wiped her eyes and nodded. She took the plant from Grandma Maisy and put it into the soil. She patted extra soil around the plant to make sure it was all secure. She stood back up next to her dad, whilst Grandma Maisy placed the butterfly next to the plant.

"We hope you are no longer in pain Rachel, and we hope you rest in peace." Grandma Maisy sniffled.

Thea leant into her dad and sobbed. The flower and the butterfly looked beautiful next to the roses. George stepped forward to say something.

"Thank you Rachel for always smiling and for always checking up on me in the shop. We will all miss your cheery self." He stepped back and wiped his eyes with a hanky.

Thea felt like she wanted to say something, but the words just wouldn't come out. She closed her eyes, composed herself and bent down to the flower.

"Goodbye Rachel." she whispered, "I will never forget you." She stood up and turned to go back to the house.

"Come on everyone." her mum chirped. "Cups of tea all around I think."

They all went and sat around the garden table. Thea wanted to go back up to her room, but she felt rude just leaving, so she sat down too.

"You chose a brilliant flower, Theadora." George complemented. "It definitely matches Rachel's personality."
"Thank you." Thea replied. She wasn't really up for a full on conversation with anyone. Thea's mum bought out a tray of tea and passed Thea a glass of lemonade. Thea's mum could tell she just wanted to be alone.
"Tee, can you come into the kitchen for a minute?"
Thea got up and made her way to the kitchen, she could see her mum was holding something.
"So, this arrived this morning, but I didn't want you to get worked up before our little service."
"What is it mum?"
"Claire sent it to me, to give to you. Rachel wrote you a letter the day before she passed away."
Thea had a weird feeling in her stomach. Rachel had actually thought of her, right up to the end of her life. She had bothered to write her a letter. She had no idea what it was going to say, she hoped it wouldn't be anything bad.
"Why don't you take it upstairs, take your drink up too."
Thea took the letter from her mum and fetched her lemonade from the garden. She ran upstairs as fast as she could, well as fast as she could go without spilling a whole glass of lemonade. She placed her drink on the bedside table and sat on her bed. She clasped the letter so tight she felt her fingers would go straight through it.
"Just open it." she said to herself. She stared at it for at least thirty seconds longer.
"Come on!" she said to herself a little louder. She ripped open the envelope and unfolded the letter. She took a deep breath and began reading.

Hi Tee,

First off, let me apologise for my writing. I am not very strong now and it is quite hard to hold the pen. Now I need to say sorry for not telling you the truth. I was too scared to tell you what was really happening because I was sick of my life just being about the cancer. People were starting to see me as the girl with cancer, and not as Rachel. You saw me as Rachel.

You became such a good friend to me and I want to say thankyou for making my last couple of weeks so amazing, you will never understand how grateful I am for that. You made me feel like my old self again. There is one more thing I need to tell you, and now I wish I had told you this in person, but I have to make sure you know.

I was always too afraid to tell you this, and I tried to hide my feelings, which wasn't easy, but I like you Tee, I like you as more than a friend.

You asked me about boys once and I told you I didn't need boys. The truth is, I don't even like boys and I was telling the truth when I said all I needed was you. I knew it when I first saw you in the shop, I thought you looked beautiful. The day you bought me the ring and I kissed you on the cheek, I wish I had just gone for the lips.

I hope what I have told you doesn't upset you, but I need you to know how special you are to me and I hope you can understand.

I am sorry I won't be there to start school with you, Tee. Be brave and be yourself, everyone will love you.

Please take care of yourself and never forget me.

Until we meet again.

Forever yours,
Rachel xxxxx

By the time Thea got to the end of the letter, she had tears streaming down her face, she could barely breathe. She couldn't believe Rachel had felt the same way about her, she hadn't just lost a friend she might have just lost her soul mate. She clutched the letter to her chest and cried and cried until she felt like she might pass out. Her mum heard the commotion upstairs and ran to Thea's room.

"Thea what is it? What's happened?" she sat down next to Thea and read the letter.

"She liked me too mum, she really properly liked me and now she will never know how I felt and I can never tell her and we could have been together and…"

"Slow down Tee, calm down, now calm down." She held Thea close.

"I am so sorry, I don't know what else I can say. At least now you know how Rachel felt, what you two had was so special, you must keep hold of that, okay?"

Thea couldn't stop crying, it felt like she had been told Rachel had died all over again.

"Mum I just want to be alone, please." Thea got under the duvet, still fully dressed and continued to cry. Her mum looked like she was about to burst into tears herself.

"I love you Thea." She left the room leaving Thea to grieve. Thea didn't know what to think, she couldn't stop crying. She just wanted Rachel.

Chapter 23

Thea stayed under the duvet for what felt like days. She closed her eyes to try and sleep, but it just wouldn't happen. Her phone was ringing and could see it was Sarah, she couldn't face that right now. A little while later it rang again, still Sarah. Thea ignored it again. She heard a phone ping, it was a message from Sarah. She dragged her phone under the duvet and read the message.

Hi Tee! I am guessing you are busy but please give me a call as soon as you are free, I can't wait to speak to you! Xx

Thea put her phone back on the bedside table, she didn't reply. She was annoyed that Sarah seemed so happy, Thea wanted to be happy, but everything was going wrong. Her mum came into her bedroom and sat on the bed. She slowly pulled down the duvet, revealing Thea's red face.

"How are you feeling, Tee?" she asked.

"How do you think I am feeling mum?" Thea groaned, not bothering to look up at her mum.

"Okay, well dinner will be ready soon, I think you need to leave this bed for a bit."

Thea turned to face her mum.

"Sorry, I am not trying to be rude, I know it's not your fault. Sarah has messaged me and she sounds all chirpy and I just can't deal with that right now."

"I understand that, I will give Sarah a ring after dinner and explain everything, if you like?"

"Yes please."

"Do you want me to tell her *everything,* or just that Rachel has passed away?"

Thea shivered. She couldn't bear to hear those words.

"You may as well tell her everything, it won't make sense otherwise I suppose."

"Not a problem, come on, let's go and eat."

Thea got out of bed, changed into her pyjamas and made her way to the dining room. Grandma Maisy had made her special pizzas, Thea had to admit, the smell was making her mouth water.

"Will you want Chinese takeaway for your birthday next week?" Thea's dad asked.

"I am not too sure yet dad, I will have a think." Thea did not want to think about her birthday, she didn't even want to celebrate it.

"Here you go, Tee." Her mum handed her a can of cola. Thea nearly drank the whole can in one large gulp. She realised she didn't even touch her lemonade from earlier.

"Have you thought anymore about…" her mum paused, realising it was not the best question to ask Thea right now.

"Thought about?" Thea asked, although she knew what her mum was about to ask.

"It doesn't matter, ignore me." her mum smiled.

"No, I have not thought anymore about the youth club tomorrow, mum." Thea said sarcastically.

"Alright, sorry."

"I just don't think I am ready to go out and pretend to be fun and smiley and just myself right now."

"It is okay, Tee. No one is going to force you to go." her dad was looking at her, reassuringly.

Thea ate her pizza and was about to head upstairs when Grandma Maisy called for her.

"Theadora, I am going to go and water Rachel's flower now the sun isn't shining right on it. Do you want to come up?"

Thea wasn't sure, she had given herself a headache from all the crying today, she knew it would set her off again.

"I will go up tomorrow Grandma, but thank you for watering it for me."

Grandma Maisy nodded and carried on towards the garden with the watering can. Thea went back up to her room and sat by the easel.

"I hope you are happy as a little fairy now, Rachel."

She wiped a tear that was trickling down her cheek. She began painting again, adding extra little flowers around the main bright orange flower Rachel was sat on.

Half an hour later, Thea's mum came in and sat on the bed.

"I have just spoken to Sarah, Tee."

Thea stopped painting and looked at her mum.

"And?" she said nervously.

"All I can say is, Tee, you have a fantastic best friend. She cried on the phone when I told her about Rachel and told me to give you a big hug from her."

"So, she wasn't mad that I made a new friend?" Thea said sheepishly.

"Of course not! She is devastated for you, Tee. You know Sarah would never be mad at you for making new friends." Thea sighed with relief.

"And what did she say you know, about me?"

"She said she is so glad you have been able to tell people about your true self. She is happy for you, we all are." her mum smiled.

Thea was so lucky to have such a great best friend as well as a supportive family.

"I will send her a message later, I am not quite ready for a phone call."

"She gets that, don't worry."

Thea went over to her mum and gave her a hug.

"Thank you, mum."

"Always happy to help, sweetheart." Her mum left the room, leaving Thea to carry on with her painting. She painted for a little longer, until her eyes began to feel heavy. She got into bed and replied to Sarah's message.

Hi Sarah, sorry I didn't answer my phone earlier. I am doing okay, my head is just a bit all over the place at the moment. I will give you a call tomorrow, thank you for being the bestest friend ever xx

Sarah messaged back straight away.

Hi Tee, please don't be sorry. I keep crying myself thinking of you being so sad, I wish I was there to cheer you up. Speak tomorrow, hugs and kisses xx

Thea read the message and smiled, she loved that Sarah was so understanding. She wished Sarah was there to cheer her up, she was brilliant at making people laugh. Thea laid down and began to think about Rachel and Sarah, she thought they would have liked each other. She started thinking about the youth club that was going to be starting tomorrow, then thought of Rachel's letter.

Be brave and be yourself. That was her decision made, she was going to go.

Chapter 24

Thea woke up to see the bright sun was streaming through her bedroom window. She sat up and immediately regretted her own decision she made last night. She knew it would be great to meet some kids her own age that were already at her new school, but what if she was the only one that didn't know anyone yet? She would be standing all sad and lonely in the corner somewhere.

"Be brave." she whispered to herself.

She got up and looked out of her window. She could see Rachel's flower, looking big and bright in the sunlight. She smiled and waved at it.

"Morning Rachel."

Thea went down to the kitchen to find her mum buttering some toast.

"Morning, Tee, how are you today?"

"I am okay thanks, I realised this morning that I can see Rachel's flower from my window."

"I thought that would be the case. Grandma Maisy planted Grandpa's rose bush there so she could see it from her own bedroom window."

"And I say goodnight to him every night." Grandma Maisy entered the kitchen smiling.

"So, I think I might go to this youth club tonight."

Thea's mum and Grandma Maisy both looked at each other and then looked over to Thea.

"Are you sure?" her mum asked. "Please don't feel like you have to because I kept pestering you about it."

"I think it would be nice to try and get to know some people before I start school. I just need to be brave."

Thea's mum's smile grew bigger.

"You have always been brave, Tee. Go get 'em!"

Thea made herself some toast and took it up to her room. She decided she was going to call Sarah whilst she felt like she could talk without crying. Sarah answered after only one ring.

"Tee! I am so glad you called, I hate to ask this, but how are you?"

"I am much better than yesterday, I couldn't stop crying at all."

"I can imagine how sad Tee. It's such a young age isn't it."

"I know. How was your holiday anyway?" Thea didn't want to keep talking about Rachel.

"The first week was great! We just hung around by the pool most days and mum actually let me try a proper alcoholic cocktail! It was gross by the way. Then at the start of the second week, mum slipped in our bathroom and sprained her ankle. She could barely walk or swim and she complained all the time."

"Oh no! What a nightmare. I tried one of dad's beers a few months ago and it was the most disgusting thing I have ever tasted!"

"Yeah, I don't get it. Maybe when you turn eighteen your taste buds just change to like alcohol."

Thea laughed. It felt good to laugh.

"I am going to a youth club tonight, I feel like it's going to be really awkward."

"Tee, you are great at making friends, you have a knack for it. It sounds like a good idea to me. I am going to be meeting up with Heather tomorrow. I'm holding secret auditions for a new friend to hang around with at school."

"That is so funny. Heather is nice though. Plus her mum always gives her treats to bring in to school, I think she's a good choice."

They both laughed loudly. It felt so good to just have a normal, fun conversation with Sarah. She really needed it.

"I better go, Tee. Mum wants me to sort out all my dirty holiday clothes, fun."

"No problem, I will let you know how tonight goes. Bye Sarah."

"Yes please do, bye Tee!"

Thea finished her toast and went over to the window. Rachel's flower was swaying slowly in the breeze, it looked like it was dancing. She decided to have a shower before getting dressed, she wanted to make sure her hair was clean for the trip out that night. She had no idea what she was going to wear, she still didn't really have an idea what teenage girls were meant to wear. She loved how Rachel dressed but she had her own style. She put on her normal baggy clothes and decided she would choose her outfit later. She went out to the garden and sat on the path next to Rachel's flower.

"Should I go tonight Rachel?" she asked, looking at the flower. She was half expecting an answer.

"What if people think I am weird?" The flower was still swaying in the breeze.

"Fine, I will go, for you." Thea giggled to herself, she would look crazy if anyone was watching her right now. She blew a kiss to the flower and went back to the house. She sat in the living room and watched some TV with her mum, who was glued to a documentary about serial killers in the United States.

"Is it normal that we love watching stuff like this, mum? Are we secretly killers?"

Her mum looked at her and laughed.

"I trod on a snail yesterday, but it was an accident and said sorry to it, I think I am okay. I can't speak for you though."

"Hey! I hate spiders but I make dad put them outside, I don't let him kill them, I think that's mean so there!" Thea poked her tongue out.

"I think we are safe then." her mum winked.

Thea watched the rest of the programme with her mum, her dad arrived home from work as it ended.

"How are my ladies?" he asked, taking off his shoes.

"Did you know mum killed a snail yesterday? Watch out dad, you could be next."

"Shut up you!" her mum threw a cushion at Thea.

"Glad to see you smiling, Tee," her dad said, grinning.

"I am going to start cooking the chicken, and no, I did not kill it myself!" her mum went off to the kitchen.

"I am going to the youth club tonight, dad."

"That's good, I'm sure you will have a great time."

"I hope so, I hope people like me."

"How can they not." he patted Thea on the head.

Thea went upstairs to choose what she was going to wear. She chose her black skinny jeans, but got stuck as soon as she had to choose a top. She went over to her dressing table where her mum had left a pile of clean clothes. There, right on top, was the white lace top. Rachel had loved that top.

Thea chose a black strappy top and put on the lace one over it. She took a deep breath and remembered how Rachel had complimented her when she first wore it.

"Dinner Tee!" her mum shouted up the stairs. Thea brushed her hair, leaving it down, and went down to have dinner. She was starting to feel nervous, she wasn't very hungry. Thea's mum noticed Thea pushing her food around her plate.

"It will be fine, Tee. If it's rubbish, just come home."

Thea liked the idea of that. She ate as much as she could and went to put on her shoes and jacket.

"Right, I am off then." The whole family was sitting, smiling at her. They all waved and wished her luck, she felt like she needed it.

She walked quite slowly, nearly turning around and going back home a few times. When she arrived at the hall, she could hear there were quite a few people in there already. A lady was standing by the door taking peoples names.

"Evening dear, can I take your name please? It is just in case we have a fire, we will need to do a register."

"No problem, my name is Thea Dixon."

"Perfect, in you go."

Thea walked in, feeling like she might be sick, it was just kids, she could do this. She noticed a trio of boys in one corner, a group of four girls in another corner and right inside the door stood two more girls.

Thea wasn't sure what to do, where to go. Before she could panic too much, one of the girls by the door tapped her on the shoulder.

"Hi! Come stand with us so you aren't on your own."

"Thank you." Thea replied.

"My name is Laura and this is Katie." The other girl stood beside Laura and waved at Thea.

"Nice to meet you, my name is Thea."

"Has your mum made you come to this thing too?" Laura sighed.

"My mum did suggest it at first, but I am going to be starting St Peters in September and I wanted to get to know some people first."

"We go to St Peters!" Katie cried. "You can walk with us on the first day of school if you like?"

Thea couldn't believe this was going so well. She didn't feel as sick anymore.

"Yes please, I would love that."

A few more teenagers arrived and the lady who was at the door began talking to everyone in the hall.

"Right everyone, before we get started, let me just introduce myself. My name is Rose and I run the youth club here, with the help of Justin and Marie." She pointed to the back of the hall where Justin and Marie were smiling and waving at everyone.

"This is a place for people to have fun and make friends, but we will not tolerate any bullying or violence. If anyone is caught doing either of these, they will be asked to leave."

"Feels like we are back at school already." Laura whispered to Thea.

"Can everyone please grab a chair and form a circle around me. This exercise will only last ten minutes and then we will leave you to do your own thing." Rose continued. A few of the boys grumbled, but eventually a circle of chairs was created around Rose. Everyone sat down, waiting to see what would happen next.

"Okay, we will go around the circle, I would like each of you to stand up, say your name and then one fact about yourself." Thea saw most of the teenagers roll their eyes.

"I know I know," Rose continued. "Let's get it done and we can move on. Let's start with you and then we will go clockwise." She pointed at a tall boy who was wearing a football shirt and had way too much gel in his hair. He stood up and said his piece.

"Hello, my name is Jack and I like to play football." He sat back down. The boy next to him looked very shy. He stood up but stayed staring at his feet and spoke very quietly.

"Hi, my, my name is Simon and I have a bulldog called Cookie."

Thea thought he was a sweet looking boy, she would love to make friends with him just so she could meet Cookie.

As a few more people spoke about themselves, Thea realised she had no idea what she wanted to say about herself. She wasn't interesting and she didn't have any pets. Katie, who was sitting next to her, stood up.

"Hey! My name is Katie, or Kate, whatever you want and I do gymnastics three times a week."

Thea thought that was impressive, she barely did any exercise. She realised everyone was looking at her, it was her turn. She thought about Rachel's letter again. *Be brave and be yourself.* She took a deep breath, stood up and smirked.

"Hi everyone, my name is Thea and I like girls."

Printed in Great Britain
by Amazon